Pierce C. Feirtear

D0994944

RETURN
TO
TROY

BLACKWATER PRESS

For Janine and Niall

First published in 1993 by Blackwater Press, Airton Road, Tallaght, Dublin 24.
Printed at the press of the publishers.

ISBN: 0 86121 404 8
British Library Cataloguing-in-Publication Data.
A catalogue record for this book is available from the British Library.
Feirtear, Pierce C. Return to Troy.
Editor: Deirdre Whelan
Cover design/illustration: Martin O'Grady, Les Quinn.
Typesetting: Professional Mac Services
Acknowledgement: E.V. Rieu for quote from translation of Homer's 'The Iliad' (Penguin Books 1950)

A number of ships had put in from Lemnos with cargoes of wine… From these the long-haired Achaeans now supplied themselves with wine, some in exchange for bronze, some for gleaming iron, others for hides or live cattle, others again for slaves…

[Homer: The Iliad]

Chapter 1

Areon rose at cockcrow while a few stars were still twinkling in a sky of softening blue. He yawned, wiped the sleep from his eyes and combed his fingers through his long, fair hair. Already he could feel that flutter of excitement, that thrill of expectation of what this day might bring – a day which promised to be like no other. Hurriedly he pulled on his tunic and laced up his sandals. Quietly he slipped out of his room.

Outside in the corridor all was shadowy and still; no one in the palace had risen yet, not even the servants. The marble of the corridor gleamed like a pale river and the row of columns were like ghostly sentries as he glided past door after door, apartment after apartment. His step quickened as he moved, for each step was bringing him closer to that secret rendezvous.

He took the small stairs – the Servants' Stairs as it was called – down to the kitchen below. Shortly afterwards he emerged through the back door into the dew-fresh air, having helped himself to a raisin-cake and stored three more, plus some fruit, in his leather bag. *"There are some advantages in living in a palace,"* he thought to himself happily.

He went out by the inner gate and moved like a thief through the courtyard garden where the violets grew. At the top of the Two Hundred Steps he paused to look down upon the city. From this vantage point on King Priam's citadel he could see all of Troy stretched out before him, so peaceful and fair on this summer's morning, so misty and yet so clear, as if everything everywhere were held in some enchanted dream. Looking now, it was hard to believe that a threat could exist, that a darkness could ever descend upon such a place, and yet.... His eyes narrowed as he turned to scan the plain beyond, down to the sea where the line of black shapes sat like sinister birds on the water. His face hardened at the sight of the Achaean ships, and the spell was broken.

It was almost ten years since those wolves of the sea had broken like a red wave on the shores of this ancient land. And for as long as Areon could remember, he had been cooped up inside this city. Not once had he been allowed set foot outside the Great Wall; not once had he walked through the fields and forests of the beloved kingdom. But today would be different. Yes, today – just for today – he and his two friends were going to be as free as the wind. With a spring in his step he began to descend.

Troy was beginning to stir from slumber as he moved through its narrow, winding streets. Over here a door opened noisily; over there a lamp showed; from a window above he heard the sound of voices. A chariot clattered by in no great hurry. Then three soldiers appeared on the street ahead, strolling to the muster. Areon fell in behind them.

"I hope you breakfasted to the full this morning," he heard the older one say to his comrades.

"Dipped bread in warm wine as usual," replied the second.

"What more?" shrugged the third.

"*What more* is right. Still, I hope you had plenty of it because you are going to need it today, men."

"Ay, it'll be a long day," said one.

"And a long march," added the other.

"The marching will be least of our worries," said the older one, and he laughed dryly.

Even the dogs in the street knew that later this morning battle would once again be joined with the enemy. *"Perhaps this time we will drive them away forever,"* thought Areon. *"If so, I'm going to be part of it, or at least catch a glimpse of it. And if not, what of it? There will be another day. At least we'll have made our first ever trip outside the Gate."*

Whistling to himself, he skipped past the soldiers and hurried along by the houses and shops.

He passed the forge, where the hammers would soon be clanging, and took a short cut across the sculptor's yard where the ground was white with marble dust. He passed the temple, and crossed the deserted square which would soon fill with the mass of Trojan soldiers and their allies.

It was some time before he came to the Great Wall and by then the entire city was awake to the din of excited cries and the beat of the marching feet. He climbed the spiral stairs of the watchtower and stepped out on to the battlements where he was to meet his friends. However, there was no sign of them there. The sun was rising steadily and soon the army would be on the move. Where were Nesa and Osban?

He turned and looked out across the silent plain to where far in the distance the dim light of camp fires still glowed. It seemed like a thousand lights were flickering out there. *"We might quench some of them today,"* he thought. *"Hector and his men will see to that."*

The sound of approaching footsteps scattered his thoughts. "What kept you?" he asked, pretending to scowl, when he saw that it was Nesa. "I've been waiting here for ages."

"You have not, you've only just arrived – I saw you from below," she replied, grinning at him. Nesa was thin, though not frail-looking. Her eyes were blue, her hair as black as a raven. Like Areon, she lived in the palace – she in the west wing, he in the east. She too had dressed this morning in the clothes of the common people.

"We would want to hurry though," said Areon "The army will be on the march soon."

"Well, you can blame Osban for any delay; that fellow is almost impossible to wake. There I was standing in the street calling up to the window – no reply. So I tossed a couple of pebbles into the room – not a stir. I could actually hear him snoring from down there in the street! In the end I had to toss a good-sized rock into the room. And that woke him, I can tell you. You should have seen the look on his face!"

"And where is he then?" shrugged Areon.

"Straggling behind as usual, he'll be here shortly."

A moment later there was the sound of heavy footsteps coming up from below. A round figure appeared at the doorway, panting. Osban was as short as Areon was tall, and as fat as Nesa was thin. With a big piece of bread in one hand and a stick in the other he plodded along the wall towards them. Areon smiled at his good friend who was always late yet never in a hurry.

"Here's a warrior who'll send the Achaeans packing," he joked.

"If they haven't left already, that is," said Nesa.

"You could have picked an easier place to meet than this, Areon," puffed their friend who looked – or was pretending to look – as if he were about to collapse. Then taking another bite of his breakfast, Osban stopped and looked innocently at his friends. "Well, what are we waiting for!" he shouted suddenly and ran past them whooping with glee.

Areon and Nesa gave chase, and the three of them raced along the battlements, rushed down the steps and ran off in the direction of the main city gate.

By now the army had begun to march. The streets bristled with numberless spears. The ground trembled under countless feet. The air echoed to a great fanfare of noise. In columns of three the foot-soldiers were moving by with short swords and round shields. Behind rode the cavalry, bronze-helmeted and crimson-cloaked. Then came a long formation of two-horsed chariots, the drivers grim-faced and erect beside proud knights who solemnly saluted the cheering crowds. On the face of every soldier was a look of steely determination. In the heart of every Trojan a flame of hope burned.

A great throng had gathered down by the Scaean Gate to see the army march from the city. Areon, Nesa and Osban pressed and pushed their way to the front of the spectators, as close as they could get to the Gate. They stood there and watched, waiting for the soldiers to appear, waiting for the opportunity to put their own plan into action.

Just then Nesa thought she heard someone call her name. In the crowd on the opposite side of the street she spotted a familiar face. "Oh look, there's Asius."

"Where? Are you sure?" asked Areon.

"Over there, and Peiros is with him. They're waving at us."

"What are they doing down here? They should be clearing out the stables," said Osban.

"Turn this way, Nesa," Areon told her. "Let on you don't notice them."

"It's no good, they know I've seen them."

"What if they follow us?" wondered Osban.

"That's not what's bothering me," said Areon. "Come on, let's slip away from here."

But before they could move, a thunderous cheer rent the air as the first soldiers came into view. The huge, sliding beams which held the gate were pulled away, and slowly, slowly it opened to release the noble sons of Troy. Then, as if the gods wished to bathe these heroes in celestial light, the early sun showered down its loving rays upon them, catching the points of a thousand spears, gleaming on the sides of a thousand helmets, transforming the whole parade into a moving river of gold. At that moment Areon wished that he too was setting out with a plume in his helmet and a sword at his side.

Almost immediately his eyes fell upon Hector, his uncle, who was leader of the army. Hector was the bravest of the brave and a lion among men. Areon was filled with admiration for him as he rode by, his armour glistening, his chariot drawn by a pair of horses as white as mountain snow. Close behind rode Areon's father, a spotted leopard's skin thrown round his shoulders, his hand resting on the silver hilt of his sword. Areon shrunk back, hoping his father would not see him here so near the Gate.

"Go on, move now," urged Nesa from behind, at the same time pushing him forward towards the open gate.

Areon froze for a moment, unsure of what to do.

"Come on Areon," said Nesa. "This was all your idea in the first place."

True, the whole venture had been set up by him. It was his plan, his idea. *"Now is no time for hesitation,"* he thought to himself. Beyond the safety of the wall lay a whole new uncertain world. It was absolutely forbidden to leave the city. But the temptation was too great.

Column after column of soldiers were passing through the Gate. Like a wave the crowd surged forward, carrying the three of them along with it.

"Here we go!" Osban cried out joyfully.

"Keep quiet," said Areon, finger to lips. "There's too many people we know around here."

"There's no stopping us now," declared his friend.

Areon could feel his feet being lifted from the ground as the milling throng swept him forward.

"Victory to the men of Troy!" the people roared with one voice.

Before he knew it he had passed through the Gate and was on the outside.

"Follow me and make sure to keep close to the wall," he immediately signalled to Nesa.

"And don't you lag behind," said Nesa, turning to Osban.

"I'm with you," smiled Osban, tossing the last little piece of bread into his mouth.

Some of the crowd followed the soldiers out the dusty road, giving them a hearty send off. Many more waved farewell from the battlements and bastions. Nobody noticed the three figures running away to the left under the shadow of the wall. Areon and Nesa dashed on, leaving Osban to scramble along behind still clutching his stick. They ran right down the length of the wall almost to where the high watchtower stood at the corner. Then crouching low they moved out, sneaking towards the cover of a few bushy olive trees. They crept under the nearest one and lay down, breathless.

They were safe, sound and out of sight. The plan was working perfectly.

Chapter 2

By and by Nesa's pulse slowed down and she sat up and peered out cautiously through the leaves. She could see the dust rising from the road and hear the distant rumble of the army on the move. The Scaean Gate was closed and the sound of cheering had died away.

"I think it's safe to move along now," she said.

"Take a hold of your reins, Nesa. I need a rest," said Osban who had heaped up a pile of leaves as a mattress and had the look of someone who was settling down for a hard-earned nap.

"We cannot wait here. You can rest as long as you like in the woods," she replied. "Now, up you get."

"Well, only if we get to build the hut there first. Remember, you promised," said Osban, glancing from one to the other.

"What do you think I have this for?" smiled Areon, producing the adze from inside his tunic.

"An axe!" enthused Osban. "That's great – where did you get it?"

"Antenor gave it to him, who else," spoke up Nesa, a little sourly.

Areon nodded. He knew that Nesa – and Osban for that matter – resented all the time he had been spending with the old carpenter recently. Instead of joining them at the stables after morning lessons he had chosen to learn the craft of woodwork. "A glutton for punishment," Nesa had called him. Still, he preferred what he was doing to what they were doing – exercising horses at no more than walking pace down in that cramped little field beside the barracks. Now, if they were allowed ride the chariots, that would be different...

"Right, let's slip away then," said Nesa, and she was gone.

"Wait, I need to show you which way to go," he called after her.

"And don't move so fast this time," pleaded Osban, lifting himself up with the help of his stick.

But his words fell on deaf ears, for Areon was bent on catching up with Nesa and there was no let up in pace until they came down to the edge of the reedy marsh which lay to the west of the great city. Luckily, it had dried up enough to make it passable. Thankfully for Osban, however, it was still sufficiently wet to hamper the progress of the race. He wiped his brow and tramped onwards, stepping into the footprints left behind by his friends.

Presently they entered the ancient wood. An early morning mist, tinged with the sun's gold, was filtering through the trees, drifting upwards and fading away into the stillness of green. They stood, hushed, wide-eyed, gazing at the trunks of the huge trees, at the glistening leaves, at the bright pearls of dew on the grass.

"Isn't it beautiful in here," whispered Nesa in awe.

"Beautiful," echoed Areon.

"Think of what we've been missing all this time," said Osban.

Nesa stretched out her arms as if to embrace the whole world. "It's so quiet and peaceful and wild and free."

"Those birds aren't so quiet and peaceful – just listen!" exclaimed Areon. In the bush opposite, what seemed like an army of sparrows was raising a terrific rumpus. All around them little blue tits were chirping merrily, springing acrobatically from twig to twig. High in the overarching branches a golden oriole called; far away, another answered. Truly, this was an enchanting place.

Nesa turned to Osban. "What are you looking at down there?" she asked.

Stretched out on the warm earth, her friend was too engrossed to hear. His eyes were fixed on a shiny black beetle – he had never seen the like of it before – fighting its way through the thick jungle of grass. When he peered more closely at it, he could see that the creature's blackness shimmered with woven bands of blue, green, purple.

"Up with you, Osban. Let's get a move on," said Areon.

Osban pulled himself up off the ground. "But don't forget we've got a hut to build," he reminded them again.

And they did as he told them. Deep in the woods they found a shady nook where they set about the task. Areon need not have brought his adze for there was plenty of deadwood lying about. They gathered the larger branches and set them against the sides of a slender silver birch; between these they now wove a thatch of ferns, covering it in completely; finally, on the inside they laid down a soft floor of grass and leaves. The result was simple but effective, and Osban was delighted.

Osban made it clear now that he wanted to stay where he was, to eat the cakes, to climb the trees and to play games for the rest of the day. He was hoping against hope, however. Nesa was neither hungry nor was she interested in playing "Warriors" or "Deerhunt", as he suggested. And Areon was determined that they explore further, insisting that they move right away because there was "something special" he wanted to show them. Only a firm promise that they would return later in the day was enough to shift Osban from his throne under the shade of the silver birch.

Off through the woods they went again, chattering and laughing as they skipped past the solemn trees, leaped over mossy logs, crashed through the undergrowth and sent animals scurrying and birds escaping before them.

Areon figured that Hector and his men would be nearing Thorn Hill by now, where they would form up in battle order. Then they would strike out across the plain, manoeuvring towards the enemy. Time was slipping away. *"If we delay too long in here, I'll miss all of the action,"* he reminded himself.

He led them along the gently rising woodland slope, until it fell away abruptly down a steep bank. There, below, exactly where Antenor had said it would be, was the stream. With a proud wave of his hand he declared: "Behold, the River Scamander."

"So this is where it begins," said Nesa.

"Well, not quite," he corrected her. "Somewhere further back there are two springs that come bubbling out of the earth – that is where it begins."

"Let's go and find them," said Nesa.

"No," said Areon, determined not to make a detour. "Let's go forward. Let's follow it and see where it goes," – though he knew where it went.

"Well, I say we should go to the springs," insisted Nesa.

"I say let's follow me!" roared Osban, making up their minds for them.

"Come back, you rascal!" they called after him.

Osban went hurtling down the slope and threw away his stick and kicked off his sandals and leapt straight into the clear, cool waters. He yelled with crazy joy to feel the cold swirl of the stream around his legs and the exquisite tingling of gravel and sand under this feet. He jumped up and down, crying out to his friends. With cupped hands he took a refreshing drink and splashed up at them a shower of crystal droplets that had them scampering back into the bushes, screaming and screeching.

But revenge was swift and sweet. The pair of them crept out and moved in on him from either side. Knee-deep in water, Osban backed away. They edged in closer, grinning, gently flicking the water towards him with their fingers. With a sudden shout they pounced and flailed madly with both hands to soak their helpless target.

Now each turned on the other. They circled and splashed, broke away and chased, tripped and fell, and rose and splashed again and again until each was breathless, exhausted and gloriously drenched.

Presently Areon pulled himself up on the bank to dry out and rest for a while. This was the life! With all the excitement he had nearly forgotten about the battle. Somehow it seemed less urgent, less important now. *"What's the point in rushing from here to there?"* he told himself. *"If we see it, we see it."*

Nor did he call on Nesa to come back when he saw her picking her way among the rocks, heading upstream.

He and Osban just lay back, basking in the sunshine like a pair of seals, listening to the stream as it tinkled over the stones and babbled past the rocks.

"Why have we waited so long to do this?" he yawned.

"I know. It was so easy to get out. Do you think we can come again soon?"

"Definitely. It's not as if it's dangerous out here anymore," said Areon. "It's been a long, long time since the Achaeans have dared to swarm up near the walls."

"Thanks to Hector and his men!"

"Just think of it, Osban. We'll soon be able to come here every day – and we won't have to sneak out either."

"Or sneak back inside," added Osban.

"And by the way, don't you worry about getting back inside this evening. I have it all worked out."

"Why should I worry? There's no one waiting for me back there… except Rinja, of course – he'll need to be fed. You should see that dog eat, he's like a wolf… No, I'm in no hurry. If I had my way, I'd go back to that hut this evening and sit outside and light a fire and maybe even settle down for the night. That would be great, wouldn't it? Out in these woods in the dark, with a big fire crackling and sparking and throwing shadows, and everything so quiet, except for maybe an owl hooting or a wild dog howling somewhere…"

"That sounds good, we must do it sometime," said Areon, but in his heart he felt deeply for his friend and thought of what it must be like for him to have to go back to that dingy little house and that flea-bitten dog, and to that cold-eyed uncle of his.

"Areon! Osban! Come up here, quickly!"

It was Nesa calling – she had found something.

At a point where the stream turned among the rocks it had formed a number of clear pools. Here Nesa had stumbled across the troughs of stone where Trojans had once washed their clothes in more peaceful times. They had been abandoned, forgotten, unused for years. Nesa was standing on one of the troughs, beaming from ear to ear.

"Look what I've found," she told them.

"That's only the washing place," said Areon, unimpressed. He had also heard about this place from Antenor.

"I know, you heard all about it from Antenor," said Nesa dismissively. "But that's not what I'm talking about. Come closer and look."

The boys stepped over quickly to look into the circular trough.

"In the name of the gods, what is that?" gasped Areon.

"It's just a stick, isn't it?" puzzled Osban, bending down closer. Then he saw the eye, the staring eye, at the top of the stick. "By Zeus, it's a snake!" he screeched and pulled away in fright.

"It's not a snake, silly," chuckled Nesa. "It's an eel, a harmless little creature."

"Doesn't look harmless to me – it's the length of my arm!"

"It's only an eel, I tell you. Come over here, it won't bite you."

"How do you know it won't?"

"No, Nesa is right," said Areon. "There's a painting of them in the palace – on the wall in Cassandra's room – am I right?"

"Correct. Come over and look, Osban. It's just a little fish."

"I'll have to take your word for it," said Osban, edging closer.

They huddled together over the trough to eye the mysterious creature. The eel seemed unconcerned. It lay motionless, staring blankly, as if in a trance.

"How did it get in there, do you think?" wondered Areon.

"Somebody might have put it there," suggested Osban.

"Maybe it just slithered in itself," said Nesa.

"No, I don't think so. It's a fish after all, isn't it, it would hardly come out of the water," reasoned Areon. "No. Either someone put it in there or it was washed in when the stream was flooded – remember the rains of last winter?"

"Maybe you're right," said Osban.

"And that means it has been in this prison for months," concluded Areon.

Osban was horrified by the thought. "We can't leave it here. You'll have to free it," he declared.

"What do you mean 'you'll'?" laughed Areon.

"Well I'm not going to touch that thing – it could bite the finger off me. You're the ones who said it was harmless – one of you should do it."

"Not me," said Areon. He grinned at Nesa. "Why not you, Nesa? After all, you found it."

"Just leave it. It will be able to slide out of the trough itself, I'm sure of it," she answered.

Again they peered down into the trough. The eel was unmoved. It opened and closed its mouth monotonously. It stared, spellbound.

"All right, let's leave it," agreed Areon, eager to move on.

They began to walk away.

But some madness inside him made Osban stop and turn back. Osban was like that, one could never be sure of what he would do from one moment to the next.

"What are you up to?" asked Nesa.

"If it bites me, I'll kill the pair of you," came the reply.

"I have to see this," said Areon gleefully.

Osban did not hesitate a moment longer. It was, he felt, a matter of either scooping the eel out of the trough or of leaving it imprisoned there forever – he simply could not allow that.

He raised his sun-kissed arms and held them over the trough. With eyes fixed on the creature, he slowly lowered his hands to the surface. He paused. "Don't stir, either of you," he whispered to his friends.

Now the hands moved again, steadily, carefully inching into the water. The eel flickered. Areon and Nesa held their breath. Then the eel moved a little to the left and stopped. But the hands were sinking and closing invisibly on the catch… closer… closer still… he had it! The hands burst from the water, clutching the frantic eel.

"Out of my way! Out of my way!" roared Osban. But the slippery eel had already wriggled out of his hands. In the wink of an eye it had slithered through the grass and into the stream. Then it shot away to freedom through the clear water. They raced along the bank to catch a last glimpse of it, but it was gone.

Yet they did not stop, they kept on running and running, and their cries could be heard echoing far across the ancient wood.

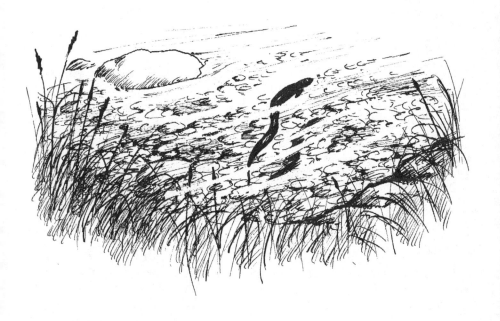

Chapter 3

"Please, let's follow on for another while," pleaded Areon. "It is not dangerous out there, believe me."

They were at the edge of the woods, sitting in long grass, looking out on the open plain once more. Close by, the Scamander was winding its way towards the sea like a snake.

"It is dangerous and you know it is," answered Nesa.

"But you can see for yourself there's not a sight or a sound of a battle out there."

"There soon will be."

"Yes, but we can stay clear of the trouble."

"Not out there, we can't."

Areon knew that Nesa would be hard to budge on the issue. He turned to Osban. "What do you think, Osban? Will you come?"

"I don't know," shrugged Osban. "I think Nesa is right. I don't think we should go much further. Anyway, I'm starving – are we going to eat or not?"

"All right. Let's only go as far as the oak tree then," Areon suggested hopefully. "We can have our food there."

"That's not a bad idea," agreed Osban, needing little persuasion.

Nesa looked at the solitary oak on the plain, some four hundred paces away. "As far as the tree but no further. That's the limit as far as I'm concerned."

The tree was a famous landmark for Trojans, not only because it was clearly visible from their lofty walls, but also because legend told that it had sprung from the earth on the day noble Ilus founded the city. It was said that the tree would stand for as long as Troy itself stood.

Keeping low, they scurried across, not daring to look up until they had reached the place.

Eagerly they stretched themselves out on the grass. Here was a happy spot for a picnic! All around them the earth was carpeted with the blue, gold and white flowers of early summer. The ageless oak towered above, its long twisted branches reaching outwards and skywards, its broad canopy of leaves providing welcome shade from the scorching sun.

They took the food from their leather wallets and laid it on the ground before them: round bread loaves, meat, portions of cheese, fruit, and the sweet cakes Areon had carried off from the palace. Nesa unslung the goatskin she had brought with her filled with cool milk. They fell upon the feast at last and not a word was spoken until the last crumb and the last drop had disappeared.

"I think we deserved that," said Nesa, satisfied. "We've come a long way today."

"I've never run so far in all my life. Mind you, I'll not be running all the way back – the pair of you might have to carry me," said Osban.

"That would be some job!" laughed Areon.

"I can hardly wait to tell Asius and Peiros where we've been today. They'll be green with envy," said Osban.

"They'll beg to be let come the next time," said Nesa.

Areon stood up. Away in the distance he could see the towers, domes and temples, and the palace that crowned them, rising out of the haze like some heavenly city. How far away Troy seemed in space and time! He unlaced his sandals. "Anyone for climbing?" he asked.

At once they were up and into the tangled web of branches. Chatting noisily, they were not to notice the strange quietness and stillness which had fallen upon the plain of Troy. It may have been due to the heat of the blazing mid-day sun or to an omen of approaching danger, but the birds had been silenced, the deer had retreated into hiding, even the delicate stalks of the long grass hung motionless in the breathless air.

Areon wanted to climb to the top of the tree or at least as high as he could go to get a proper view of the countryside. His two friends, however, were content just to clamber out to a perch on one of the sturdy branches lower down.

"I'm sorry I didn't bring Rinja with me," said Osban. "He would have loved it in the woods and out here in the open."

"That old bag of bones would never have made it this far," joked Nesa.

"He would so. And I'll tell you something: next time we come out here Rinja is definitely going to be with us."

"Well, I hope you threw him a bone before you left this morning."

"I did, I looked after him well this morning. Not that I needed to – Rinja is well able to look after himself."

"I have to agree with you there," said Nesa. "Old Rinja knows each and every scrap heap in the city of Troy!"

"You are so funny," retorted Osban.

Nesa peered upwards through the leafy branches. "Areon, what are you doing up there?" she called. "It's about time we started thinking of heading back."

The battle-curious Areon had almost pulled himself to the top. Only now did he become aware of the eerie silence that enveloped him. However, his eyes could tell what his ears could not hear. Through the haze away to the west he detected the sign of movement. The rising cloud of dust was unmistakable. Areon could not but notice that the storm of dust was growing larger, spreading wider and – what was quite disturbing – it appeared to be approaching at an alarming rate.

"Come on, Areon," called Nesa again from below.

"We want to go back to the woods to the hut," added Osban. "It's getting late."

But he scarcely heard their words. And now he could hear the noise. It started first as a distant rumbling, like a soft roll of drums across a valley or the muffled roar of thunder out at sea – a dull, trembling sound, but gradually becoming louder and louder, as if the whole earth was groaning under some deep burden of pressure or pain. With an awful clarity he could now see the whirling shapes of riders amidst the turmoil of dust. The storm of battle had been unleashed.

A sudden knowledge of danger gripped him. It was time to leave this place, and fast. He wanted no part of any battle. In a hot panic he began to descend. But already it was too late.

Like heavy storm-clouds that gather unexpectedly on the horizon of a summer's day and surge like a wave across the peaceful meadows, sending the farmer running for cover, drenching the cattle, scattering the corn, darkening everything, so the terrible battle-wave of war crashed down upon the plain of Troy. The ground shook and the air echoed to the clash of bronze and the cries of men. Fury went on the rampage as riders on horses, horses without riders, warriors in chariots swept in madly around them. Chariot smashed into chariot and over-turned... One warrior was struck by a bronze-pointed spear and fell to the ground. Another howled like a wolf as he swung a great axe through the air. Another desperately raised his shield to fend off a blow. The sky teemed with arrows. Horses bolted violently. Dark death stalked through the tempest...

Too horrified to look, Areon, Nesa and Osban clung to the tree. They waited and waited, praying for the storm to pass. And after what seemed like an eternity, it did pass – the roar of battle faded away, the dust began to settle on the plain again. Even when the silence had returned they still waited.

Thoughts raced through Areon's mind. Would the soldiers return? Was there anyone still out there? Was it safe to move? He could see his friends huddled together in the branches below him. Frozen by fear, they were as still as statues in the deafening silence.

He waited a little longer. It must be safe to move now, he thought. They could crawl on their hands and knees back to the woods where they would be safe. They should never have left the cover of the trees, he knew that now.

He beckoned to his pals but they did not notice him. Then he whistled softly, but was not heard. Just as he was about to lower himself on to the branch below, he heard the sound of chariot wheels. Once more a bolt of fear shot through him.

There were three of them, two in the chariot, the other on horseback. The horsehair plumes of their bronze helmets immediately identified them as the enemy. One of them appeared to be wounded, for he stumbled from the chariot and fell to his knees doubled up in pain, yet still clutching his sword. His two comrades quickly came to his assistance, removing his weapon and

stretching him out on the soft earth under the tree. He lay there and groaned in pain, crying out to the gods. All the while, Areon peeped down, his heart thumping madly.

A moment later a second chariot drawn by a pair of black horses sped up to the tree. The charioteer reined in wildly to a halt. A small but broad, muscular man leapt off. In one hand he held a blood-stained sword, in the other a round, leather shield. Areon saw at a glance the hideous figure drawn on that shield – a three headed monster with awful staring eyes and hair writhing with snakes. This was a cruel man.

"What is going on here? Pick up your weapons, there's a battle to be fought!" he shouted at the soldiers.

"But, your lordship, my friend..." pleaded the young soldier.

"Your friend will look after himself," roared the man. "Leave him. Get up on your horse, soldier. Now!"

The first soldier jumped to his feet. The second turned away slowly, hesitating to leave his wounded friend.

"Move it! Move it!" bellowed the man with red rage.

It was at that very instant that poor Osban lost his grip and fell. Down he came tumbling through the branches, almost knocking the man off his feet. The Achaean let out a startled cry, then seized the luckless boy by the belt of his tunic, dragging him roughly up off the ground.

"Now what have we got here? A young Trojan pup I'll bet!"

The panic-stricken boy glanced up and saw the small beady eyes glaring at him, saw the white boar's tusks on the rim of the leather helmet, saw the rough beard, the misshapen nose and the battle-scar on the man's cheek.

"Spying on us, were you?" He pushed the boy to the ground and pulled him up again.

Suddenly there was a rustling of branches as Nesa swung down from the tree. She charged at the Achaean, beating him with her fists.

"Leave him alone you brute! Leave him alone! Take your hands off him!" she screamed. The Achaean only laughed – a cruel, cold laugh – and grabbed Nesa by the scruff of the neck.

"Another one!" he howled. "Falling like chicks from the nest."

"Look, my lord Megnor," called the other soldier, who had stepped back and was pointing up high into the tree.

Areon's heart sank. He knew that the game was up and was already climbing down through the gnarled branches of the ancient oak tree.

Chapter 4

Once again the crimson sun was awakening from the River of the Ocean on which it sailed around the world. There was a strong wind blowing; purple clouds came scudding across the skies and gulls wheeled in close to the rocky shore. From headland to headland across the bay the Achaeans had drawn up their ships in rows. There were hundreds of them, their hulls pitch-black, the bows blood-red, their sterns raised high like the horns of bulls.

A solitary vessel rested on the shore. She had arrived from Lemnos the evening before with cargoes of wine. That the merchants of that island kingdom had begun trading with the enemy was a source of deep anger to the Trojans. Her crew were sitting around a fire on the beach, waiting for their captain to return. They were growing impatient:

"Is he ever coming?"

"It's a shame to be wasting precious time, with a wind like that to fill our sails."

"The sooner we pull away from this place the better. There's been too much trouble already, and there will be more, mark my words. I have a bad feeling about it."

"And our ship, sitting here like a duck in the water."

"Steady on, steady on. Are you mice or men?" the helmsman gently mocked them. "Your captain is settling matters. He will return in due course. We will depart in good time. The day is long. The wind will carry us. What problem is there?"

The men muttered into their wine cups and glanced once more towards the Achaean camp, only a sling-shot away. From where they sat they could see the damage done to the defensive wall under the recent Trojan counter-attack. Had they come closer they would have seen the deep trench that bristled with the shafts of broken spears and arrows. Closer still and they would have seen the inner circle of huts where the wounded lay.

Beside one of these huts their captain stood talking with the Achaean warlord. Terms for the sale of the wine had been finally agreed. They were bargaining now over other matters and once more the conversation was becoming heated.

"You have been handsomely paid for your wine – too handsomely. Now you want to steal the tunics off our backs as well. I'll not have dealings with the likes of you again," said the one with the helmet of the boar's tusks.

"With respect, my lord, it is you who are being unreasonable. I am prepared to carry your messenger, to safeguard and deliver your booty to your kingdom, and to return from there immediately with the supplies and the men your lordship requests. Furthermore, I must await the rest of my payment until I do so. For all of this, I merely seek a fair reward."

"Fair reward!" scoffed the Achaean. It galled him to have to bargain with these grubby merchants. But he had no choice. The Trojans were on the offensive, making desperate attempts to break the siege. He needed reinforcements urgently, he wanted his treasures safely out of the way, he could not spare the men – not to mention the ship – to do it. Another time, another place and he would not even allow this fellow to stand in his shadow. "All right, this is my final offer. In addition to what I have already agreed, I will give eight talents of gold and three of my finest cauldrons, untouched by fire. Nothing more."

"It is done," the captain accepted.

"And you will also transport the slaves?"

"Just three of them, you say?"

"Yes," nodded Megnor.

"Agreed."

The Achaean turned and walked away. The man from Lemnos heaved a sigh of relief. He was anxious to get back to sea.

The young Trojans were taken from the prison-hut and led away. Heads bowed, they walked in silence. Flanked by a pair of footsoldiers, they were marched down to the water's edge. They were ordered to climb aboard the ship and made sit in the cramped space between the large storage jars and the rowers' bench.

Shortly afterwards, the sea captain appeared, accompanied by another Achaean – the warlord's messenger – a tall, thin man in a dark cloak. Behind them in pairs came the soldiers bearing the wooden chests. A muffled cheer rose from the sailors on the beach. They stamped out the fire and leapt on board.

The Achaean seemed disgruntled, unhappy at the prospect of the voyage. The captain, though, was in high good humour. He took a wine jug and poured two cups, offering one to the man. He spoke: "To the Heavenly Ones, that they may look down with favour upon us. To Poseidon, the Earthshaker, that he may safeguard us on the wine-dark sea." He tilted his glass and poured a drink-offering to the gods on to the ground. The Achaean did likewise. "To our friends and kind hosts, the noble men of Achaea. May they rise and vanquish their foe. May the victory be theirs," said the captain.

The Achaean nodded. Both men drank, emptying their cups. The captain now called to his crew:

"Zeus has sent a favourable wind to speed us on our way. Let us not delay. Set up the mast."

At once the men lifted the mast of pine and set it upright in its box. Others began securing their oars in the leather straps. Then they pulled easily, just a few strokes to take the vessel away from the sandy shore.

"Spread the sails," ordered the captain.

"Spread the sails," echoed the helmsman.

They hoisted the white sail. Struck full with the wind, it swelled out and the ship surged forward. She sliced through the waves and moved rapidly out across the bay.

So powerful was the wind behind them that once they had cleared the headland it was no longer necessary to row. It was not often sailors had such luck – the gods had indeed smiled upon them. Heartily the men began to sing:

Far away from the mainland green
Where the farmer harvests in the field
Where the shepherd sits upon the rock
Where slowly stirs the grazing flock.

Like a runaway horse, the ship was racing out to sea. White waters rushed past her bow. Seething waves surged in her wake. Areon sat up and looked back. He saw the land, his homeland, falling away astern: he felt his spirit sink and withdraw deep within him. His palms were wet, his mouth was dry, his stomach churning like the seas that surrounded him. He who had wanted to escape Troy – how he wished now he could be safe inside her walls! He who had led his friends to this – how could he ever forgive himself?

> Far out on the foaming sea
> Where big waves roll and wild winds blow
> Where seabirds will not dare to go
> The cresting ship goes running o'er

Osban was deaf to the sailors' song, blind to the lurching ship and dead to the salty spray that soaked him. All he could think of was Rinja. Only Rinja. His mind went back to that first day when his father came home with the little pup. That was the year before he had lost both his father and his mother, one to the war, the other to fever. But that day he was happy. He remembered how the pup had whimpered that night when they left it in its box, and how he had felt sorry for it and taken it to his bed. He had woken the next morning to find the dog waiting beside his pillow – just like Rinja would be waiting for him now! But who would come for him? Who would care for him?

> Skies may darken, winds may blow
> Waves may rise with mighty show
> With a mountain above, a valley below
> But the cresting ship goes running o'er
> The cresting ship goes running o'er

Nesa though, was taking stock of the situation. Shortly after her capture she had realized that they would probably be sent away as slaves. Slavery was a "fate worse than death itself" she had heard Trojans say. Still, there was no point in crying over spilt milk, she told herself. The voyage would be a long one, yet she was determined to note every turn they made, every island they passed, every headland they rounded or any other land-mark they met. She clenched her fists and sat and watched.

Spectacular sailing progress was made throughout the day. By early evening land appeared on the horizon. Then the wind abated somewhat and so the crew took to the oars again.

Bright stars were twinkling and the crescent of the moon was high above as they brought their vessel in to rest on a pebbly beach. Quickly they furled the square sail, let down the forestays, dropped the mast and cast the anchor. Each man jumped happily on to the sand.

In no time a crackling fire was burning and hungry hands were dividing the food. Areon, Nesa and Osban were given water, a little bread and some fish and put sitting twenty paces away. They were thrown a couple of blankets and told to settle down for the night.

They sat there gloomily, scarcely nibbling the food. A long silence passed between them.

"Fat lot of trouble you've got us into," said Nesa at last.

Areon did not reply. Back in the prison-hut she had given him a roasting over what had happened. She was still furious with him. "'We'll just go to the oak tree and no further', – I should have known better than to listen to you," she threw at him.

"Would you ever drop it, Nesa. There is no point in this," spoke up Osban.

"Fine. That's the last I'll say of it. But just remember, Areon, to listen to my advice next time you get one of your bright ideas."

Areon nodded, biting his lips and accepting the truce.

Around the campfire the sailors ate their fill and drank from brimming bowls of wine. One or two were already stretched on the warm sand, asleep.

"That lot will be snoring soon," whispered Osban. "Why don't we try to slip away during the night?"

"And go where?" shrugged Nesa. "We are in the middle of nowhere, we don't know where we are or who or what is out there. How could we ever get back home?"

Areon nodded in the direction of the ship. "We could try and take that," he suggested.

"Impossible," said Nesa.

Areon did not push this idea any further. He thought it wise for the time being to stay quiet and listen to what Nesa had to say.

She pulled a blanket up around her shoulders and drew in close to her two friends. She looked intently at one and then the other. "We have no choice right now but to do whatever they say and to go wherever they take us. And when we get there we sit and wait."

"Sit and wait for what?" asked Osban, puzzled.

"For our people to find out where we've been taken and to pay enough gold to have us returned. It's as simple as that. It's been done before, hasn't it?"

"For some people it has," said Areon.

"Yes, for people like you – your family is rich. Who'll pay my ransom?" demanded Osban, eyes aflame.

"Our people will bring you home as well, Osban, I promise. No, the problem is that nobody at home knows that we went outside the walls! But soon they are bound to discover what has happened to us," said Nesa.

"What if they don't?" asked Osban in desperation.

"They will, believe me."

"What if they don't? What if they never find out? And even if they do, how are they going to bring us home? It could take years – years!"

And so they sat on the lonely beach and comforted each other.

The sailors from Lemnos were quiet now. The glowing embers of the fire were beginning to fade. Small waves lapped on the shore. Above them, the night sky was bright with a thousand twinkling stars.

Chapter 5

Dawn came early, the grumbling sailors rose. Without delay they boarded their vessel and spread the sail once more. This time they did not make for the open seas but instead kept close to the coast. The sky was clear, the wind was good and all the long day they sailed. At night they came ashore again to rest.

For three days they sailed downwind, chasing the sun until they came to the place which Nesa was to remember as "the point of turning". A chain of high mountains was the distant landmark that eventually led them to a headland of grey rock jutting out into the sea. It was a place well known and feared by the sailors. Doubling the headland meant turning the ship almost right around, so that the northern wind which had borne them so swiftly across the ocean now abruptly became an enemy against which they would have to row. Many a good ship had been wrecked here in the past. Others had been blown away off course, sent drifting into nameless waters, never to return.

The sailors had every reason to be fearful. The wind was blowing fiercely. The sea was in turmoil, with short waves running in every direction at once, slapping against the ship.

Gritting their teeth, the men from Lemnos thrust oars to the water and fought to turn their ship around. She began to roll awkwardly from side to side. Salty spray came splashing on to the deck. For one awful moment it seemed as if the faltering ship might not match the windswept sea.

"Helm to port! Steady on the starboard!" shouted the captain.

"Are you men or mice?" roared the helmsman, his face now set in granite.

"Move those oars. Move those oars, I said. Pull! Pull!" the captain was bellowing.

The rowers answered the call well. Their faces contorted with the strain, they pulled mightily as one team, throwing up the water with their oars. Slowly the ship swung round to her new course. She edged forward, victorious. The captain mopped his brow with relief – a perilous obstacle had been overcome. It would be a straightforward run from here.

So it was. Steadily and uneventfully, they advanced along the coast.

On the morning of the sixth day they encountered a thick bank of fog. The captain seemed unconcerned, however. It drifted down upon them, billowing like white smoke as if a mysterious fire was burning somewhere over the horizon. Sea, sun, land, everything was soon obscured; all was wrapped in the silent mist. Areon, Nesa and Osban were drifting too on their own sea of silence. They too were wrapped in a cloud. The oars creaked. The oars splashed. They sat as if hypnotised.

Quite suddenly the fog cleared. The helmsman sprang to his feet.

"I see the island," he called out pointing ahead of him.

Every oarsman turned to look.

"It's there, don't fret, it won't disappear. Keep your hands to the oars," the captain told them.

Areon woke up out of his trance and craned his neck to view. Sure enough a lofty island had appeared on the starboard side, close to the mainland. It rose out of the blue sea like some fantastic beast sculpted in rock. Green, dappled with white, was its colour; and its form was that of a lion – a stalking lion that crouches unseen, poised to strike down its luckless prey. Gazing at it, Areon felt a shiver run down his spine.

The oarsmen rowed again with fresh vigour. They chatted happily, joked and laughed. Even the Achaean in the long cloak seemed more relaxed; he smiled for the first time, if a little weakly.

The captain began to pace up and down the length of his ship, calling to his crew: "Good... no slackening... put your backs into it... Shortly you will have all the food and drink you want, plenty of rest and a soft bed for the night... You've done well, you've done well, men." He stopped before Areon. He thrust his hand into his tunic and produced an apple. "Here, son, take it," he said, tossing the fruit to the startled boy.

Areon took it, muttering something.

The captain laughed: "What is this, not a word of thanks? I've a lad just like you at home in Lemnos – never any gratitude. He'll be sailing with me one of these days. Oh yes, the sea will cure him of his laziness – if not his ingratitude!" And he laughed again. "Tell me, boy, are you a lazy one too? I hope you are not. They will not take too kindly to lazy fellows on the Island of Leucas." He took out two more apples. "Here, give these to your friends," he said and walked away.

Areon might have thanked him then but was held back. *"How can you expect thanks from me – you who has carried us away as slaves?"* he thought. *"No, not even if you offered me three baskets of fruit, or ten, or a hundred. I'd rather thank a snake for the bite it gave me!"*

And so they sailed past the great rump of white cliffs on the southern end of the island; continued on by the thickly wooded flank – there was not a sign that anyone lived there; and rounded the rocky north-eastern headland that stretched like a claw into the sea.

Then a different picture met their eyes: jagged coast gave way to sandy beach: wooded hill tapered down to grassy plain. High on a solitary hill stood a fortress of stone, keeping a watchful eye over land and sea. Gathered beneath were clusters of houses and huts, forming a small town. Town and fortress were to each other as servant and master: the one, humbled and low; the other, proud and over-bearing.

As they rowed in towards the island three horn-blasts sounded above the waves.

Nor was it easy to manoeuvre the ship into the narrow channel that separated the island from the mainland. The entrance was almost cut off by a long sand bar and the waters were so shallow there was the very real danger of running aground. The captain went to the bow and peered down anxiously. Signalling caution with one hand, urging movement with the other, he edged his ship into position, eased her forward and brought her through the gap. Then he made a sharp right-handed turn to the island's harbour.

Nesa sat up, wide awake and alert. She could see the Achaean soldiers standing on the wooden jetty, waiting for the ship. She spotted the group of women and men, and the children who watched with a burning curiosity. In her hand she held three carved beads of amber, threaded with a thin wire of gold, which she had kept hidden from her captors. They were a gift from her mother, and her hope had been to collect enough of them to one day make a beautiful necklace of amber and pearl. Now these hopes had been dashed. But that would not be the end of it, she told herself. Fingering and kneading the beads into her palm, she vowed that one day she would return to complete it. And with that she clenched them in a fist.

The shouts of the sailors mingled with the happy cries of children as the ship pulled in. The Achaean and the captain climbed ashore to be greeted by the officer in charge. The three of them walked briskly down the jetty to where the chariots were waiting. They were driven away.

"Where's he off to now?" groaned one of the crew.

"Gone to have another little chat, I suppose," muttered another.

"I wager he'll disappear for the rest of the day," another said.

They turned to the helmsman, but he was already curled up in the corner, nodding.

"If he thinks that we are going to sit here waiting for him to return, he's got another thing coming," said the first one boldly.

"Ay," answered the rest in one voice.

Time slipped slowly by. The onlookers began to drift away in twos and threes. The crew complained; however, none of them dared to stir until their captain returned.

Finally, he reappeared. He told them:

"All is arranged. You may unload."

The sound was music to their ears. As fast as they could they lifted out the great storage jars, some empty, some full of wine. Then they took a quantity of copper and tin ingots, some ivory, glass and a few logs of ebony. Lastly, they hauled up the wooden chests. Their work was done; they were happy; a few days rest were beckoning. Each man snatched one or two belongings, jumped from the ship and with quickening steps walked off down the jetty. The Achaean soldiers departed also, bringing the goods with them.

Before he left, the captain turned to them: "You must stay where you are. Someone is coming for you. I wish you well," was all he said. Then he too walked away.

Nesa watched him ride off in his chariot and disappear. They were all alone. She stood up, yawned and stretched herself. "It's so cramped here. If only we could get off this rotten ship. My back is aching. My knees hurt. I'm absolutely exhausted," she sighed.

"Areon, please give me one of those apples now, I'm famished," said Osban.

Areon seemed lost in thought and did not hear him.

"Areon, throw me an apple, will you?"

Areon tossed him the fruit. "Do you want yours, Nesa?"

"No, I can't eat it, you keep it."

Osban devoured his apple. Areon looked at his, took one bite of it and threw it away in disgust. "Nice of the captain to think of us," he spat out bitterly.

"He's such a decent fellow, that captain," mocked Osban. "I do not know how we can ever repay him."

"I know how to repay him," said Areon. Suddenly he had taken out his adze and was brandishing it.

Nesa turned and saw the fire in his eyes. "Put it away," she advised.

"How did you manage to keep it?" asked Osban, surprised to see the tool.

"I kept it well hidden – that's how," said Areon and in the same breath he had it above his head, brought it down and struck the bench in front a splintering blow. He struck again, a second, a third time.

"Stop it, you're mad!" cried Nesa, alarmed by the reckless-ness of it.

Areon was not listening though. Blindly, he hacked and chopped at the wood. "I'll show him what I think of him and his ship!" he raged, caring little about the noise being made, caring less about the damage being done.

"Areon, stop this foolishness!" demanded Nesa.

He was beside himself now. He stood up, grabbed one of the oars and threw it into the water. He kicked at one of the storage jars, knocking it over. He struck out wildly with the adze again and waved his fist. Finally, he just threw himself down on the deck, exhausted. Only then did his bitter tears begin to flow.

His friends had scarcely time to lay a hand on his shoulder, and to raise the fallen jar, when Nesa heard the sound of cart-wheels.

"Put the adze away – there's someone coming," she told him.

A mule-cart drew up near the jetty. Its driver came ambling towards them. He was a big, grey-haired, long-bearded, poorly-dressed man. He walked with a peculiar kind of shuffle, the arms folded behind his back, shoulders crouched and the head bent low as if he were looking for something on the ground. He strolled to the edge of the jetty and beckoned them to come to him.

"I wonder who this fellow is?" whispered Osban.

"He doesn't look like an Achaean," said Nesa. She turned to Areon who was sitting there, head down. "Are you all right? Come, we must go."

Feeling relieved, but at the same time apprehensive, they climbed up out of the ship.

They had nothing to fear from this man, however, for the eyes that met them were warm and friendly. Pointing to himself, he only said: "My name is Andraemon. Come with me," and turned and walked back down the pier.

They followed him at once.

Chapter 6

By now it was evening, the island people had gone to their homes. The swineherd named Andraemon took the Trojan captives out the long and winding road which led to his homestead. They passed under the shadow of the fortress on the hill, and skirted the town beneath it. They passed the silent vineyards and olive groves and the sun-ripened fields of wheat and barley. They passed through the meadow where a shallow river flowed, and on through pastures where cattle grazed.

Finally they came to the woodland track leading to his dwelling place. A pair of huge hounds came bounding towards them, followed by a much smaller dog. They rushed to their master with much fawning and tail wagging. "Go on, be off with you," called Andraemon with a friendly wave of his hand. "You'll be fed soon enough."

They rode up then to a humble cottage built of stone and roofed with a thatch of rushes. Beside it stood a hut made of planks of deal. And next to this was a large walled-in yard containing sties for the swine. One look about the place and Nesa could tell that this was not the home of a freeman.

"You must be hungry, my young friends – let us prepare the food," said Andraemon, and he leapt eagerly from the cart.

Areon was asked to kindle the fire, while Nesa was sent to collect more firewood and Osban to fetch the water. The swineherd threw some thick brushwood on the ground and laid goatskins on top for them to sit on. Next, he went and brought out some meat which he sliced and placed on the spit. It was soon roasting, and their mouths watered.

The bread was passed around and the cups were filled. Generous portions of meat were given and white barley-groats sprinkled on top. Each one fell to the feast with zest.

When they had eaten and drunk their fill, Andraemon invited his guests to tell their tale. Areon, who was feeling much better in himself now, was the first to speak. He told of Troy and of the war; talked of his plan on that awful day, how they had slipped out the Scaean Gate, and played in the woods, and followed the stream, and gone to the oak on the plain; he described the battle and spoke of their capture by Megnor though he made no mention of a certain person's fall from the tree, much to the culprit's relief.

All this time Andraemon listened attentively, and by the time Areon was finished it was dark. The fire hissed softly, melting into the silence. The swineherd shook his head and sighed:

"Your misfortune has been great – it grieves me to hear of it."

"You have also shared such misfortune?" probed Nesa.

He looked up at her. "Yes, and so have others, many others. You are not alone in this... I too have stood chained in a line in the market place and listened as they haggled over the price of my head... that was on the island of Delos a long time ago. I remember it as if it were yesterday. You know of this place of course?"

Nesa nodded. "It is the birthplace of Apollo, son of Zeus. You will find there the Sacred Lake where the goddess, Leto, bore him."

"My father journeyed once to Delos to consult its oracle," said Areon.

"Yes, for Trojan and Achaean alike it is sacred ground – I understand this. But for the slave, Delos and its market place is a thing cursed forever," said Andraemon.

"How did they take you?" inquired Nesa further.

Before he answered her, the swineherd stirred up the embers and threw another log on the fire. "Twenty years ago and yet it seems just like yesterday…" he began. "My home was in a place called Paddan Aram, far far from these shores. We had a good life there my wife and I: our land was good, our cattle well-fed. Our two children were my greatest joy. Timna was six, Hushan only two. All day long they would play in the fields, running this way and that, tugging at my sleeves. And in the evening they would curl up and fall asleep at my feet…" As he spoke, the memory of his dear ones rose up before him like a searing flame, filling his voice with a trembling emotion. But he composed himself and continued:

"The story of my capture is simple. One day – it was in the spring – a messenger arrived from my father with the news that I was to come to him at once. I left immediately and rode all day until I arrived at Ramasheda, the place of my birth. There my father told me of the dispute which had arisen between him and my younger brother. They had had a blazing row – about what, it matters not – and my brother had left his father's house, vowing never to return.

"I went to find my brother, to bring him home if I could. Finding him proved more difficult than I expected. A long search over mountain and valley eventually brought me to the edge of the great sea. In a little fishing village I finally met someone who had seen my brother, – a merchant who told me that I would find him in the town of Ugarit, four days journey away. It was the news I had waited for and my heart was glad.

"But Fate conspired against me. I was approached by a sailor – a snake if ever there was one! – who offered me passage to Ugarit. His price was reasonable; the trip by sea would be quicker, easier: I accepted his offer. So I left my tired horse in good hands and like a guileless fool boarded his boat. No sooner had we left the harbour behind than this loathsome creature and his friends set upon me. They took my purse of silver; tore the ring of gold from my finger.

"The rest you know. Brought to Delos, I was stripped of my cloak and fine tunic; given vile rags to wear. Then they sold me like an animal. I was given the name 'Andraemon' – a fine Achaean name," he added bitterly.

Osban was about to ask him his real name, but held his tongue. Nesa wanted to question him about Megnor, and about the fortress on the hill, but before she could do so, Andraemon stood up, abruptly. He said: "The hour is getting late and the night is short. You must have your rest. They will be sending for you at first light. Come with me."

He brought them to the little hut next to the cottage and gave them blankets of wool for their beds. Then he left them, returning to keep vigil beside the camp fire.

Nesa shook her head. "Imagine, that poor man has been a slave these past twenty years."

"That's twice as long as the War. How does he bear it? They'll not hold me here for twenty years," said Osban.

"I hope not," shuddered Areon.

"I promise you not," said Nesa.

They laid the blankets on the ground and made themselves as

comfortable as they could. Too tired to worry, or even think of what tomorrow might bring, all they wished for at this moment was rest. Before Areon went to sleep there was something he wanted to say to his friends: "About today, on the ship, I am sorry for what I did. It was very stupid of me."

"It was, " said Nesa, but in a kind way.

"At least you did some damage while you were at it," joked Osban. "I hope the captain notices it – serves him right."

"Well, I am sorry," said Areon.

"Forget all about it," said Nesa softly. "Let us get some sleep."

Nor were they long in entering the land of their dreams, each falling into a peaceful slumber that washed away the tiredness, soothed their aching limbs and eased the sorrowful burden of their hearts.

But the night was short, too short.

Chapter 7

At the crack of dawn Andraemon came hurrying into the hut to rouse them. Gently he shook Nesa awake: "You must rise immediately. The soldiers are waiting outside. Make haste."

Osban crawled out from under his blanket. Areon sat up, yawning. Through the small open window he could see three, perhaps four men in the yard, the plumes of their helmets rippling in the breeze.

"Hurry along, my friends," Andraemon urged them, "and remember, do everything you are given to do and do it well. Never dawdle and do not be seen to be idle. When you bow your head, make sure to bend the knee as well – it is best that way, you will see, they will accept you and will not make your life here too miserable. And here, take this, it'll keep you going." He thrust into Nesa's hand some food wrapped in cloth. For this, later in the day, they were to be grateful.

"What about Areon? Is he not coming also?" asked Osban, as he and Nesa were led to the door.

"No. I am told he is to remain. They have different plans for him."

Osban glanced at Areon and shrugged. Before Areon knew it his two friends were gone. He did not know when he would see them again.

"We have to get a move on, my young man," said Andraemon to Areon. "Calchas orders that you must tend the king's sheep. I am to bring you to them."

"Who is this Calchas?"

"Calchas is the king's right-hand man, the one who sailed on the same ship as you – with important messages from Lord Megnor, no doubt."

"And Lord Megnor?"

"Megnor is the old king's son."

"I see."

"And a nasty pup and scoundrel if ever there was one. Of course, I need hardly remind you of this," said Andraemon.

"That is so," replied Areon.

"Well, let us be on our way then," continued the swineherd. "I have decided to let you have my best dog, Teg. He may not be big, but he's clever. More importantly, he knows how to deal with sheep. And he'll be a good companion for you up there."

"Up where?"

Andraemon looked earnestly at the young Trojan. "I am ordered to take you to a certain valley in the hills. It is not too far away, and I will try to see to it that you come back here every now and then to visit your friends. I promise you that."

"You mean I must remain there day and night?"

"I'm afraid so."

Areon felt crushed by this last piece of news. Was it not bad enough to be torn away from family and homeland? Was it not bad enough to be thrown into slavery without now being isolated from his friends as well and forced to live alone on some alien hillside? Fate, it seemed, had dealt him yet another blow. Shaking his head, he followed Andraemon out the door.

The swineherd gathered some provisions for the unwilling shepherd and secured them to the mule. They set out without delay.

The sun was above the hills, lightening the blue emptiness of the sky, clasping every living thing in its warm embrace. Across the deeper-blue waters below came a cooling breeze which stirred the grass and rustled the leaves. There was a faint fragrance of pine in the air. Stepping lightly, Andraemon led the mule over the stony hillside track, with Teg moving dutifully at his side. The young Trojan plodded along behind, panting as he tried to keep up, for his limbs were heavy, his heart heavier still.

The path wound its way up to the left of a towering outcrop of white rock, towards a solitary tree standing at the sky's rim. The final climb to the top was steep and difficult. There Andraemon stopped at last to allow Areon catch his breath. He pointed to the south:

"We cross the plateau for a stretch. Do you see the pair of hills beyond? – over there to the right. In the valley between you shall find your sheep."

"How many?" inquired Areon.

"About forty in all, mainly ewes and lambs. The rest have been brought to mountain pastures," said Andraemon, gesturing towards the cloud-touching peaks in the distance.

"At least I do not have to go there," thought Areon. It was a cold comfort, however.

"Our first task must be to gather them, count them and pen them. No doubt a few will have strayed over the hills – there's always one or two contrary fellows! – they can be taken care of tomorrow. And, let us not forget, we must find somewhere for you to live."

Areon looked to the horizon with uneasy eyes. Already the prospect of facing into a lonely night was looming darkly ahead. Another thing was troubling him. He asked straight out:

"Is there anything to fear from the wild beasts in these parts?"

The swineherd chuckled. "No, my young friend, you will have nothing to fear. Like everywhere else, during the lambing time eagles can be a menace: the shepherd must be vigilant then. Other than that, the sheep may graze peacefully all day long and rest peacefully all night... I have heard it said, though, that some years ago a wolf had the misfortune to cross over from the mainland, foolhardy creature that he was." Andraemon quietly laughed again. "He did not live long enough here to satisfy his appetite, I can tell you."

It was not long before they reached the place. The valley was shallow but sheltered, rocky but grassy enough for the sheep that were in it. The flock was well scattered: some were feeding in twos and threes along the edges of the stream below; some were to be seen among the bushes and trees of the opposite hillside; others were but dim white dots on the bare slopes a long way off.

"Take Teg with you and begin the gathering. Start with those furthest down the valley. I'll set to work here," Andraemon told him.

Areon whistled to the dog, who ran to him as if he knew well the mission in store. He had to smile at the sight of this eager little fellow, a most unusual-looking dog, all white except for a most startling black patch on the left eye, and with a short little tail that always seemed to be twitching and moving. "Come, Teg, we'd better hurry," said Areon.

Hastening also, Andraemon took up a sharpened axe and began cutting down some thorny bushes with which to make temporary pens for the animals.

Bringing home the king's sheep proved easier than Areon had expected. It was all down to Teg. At a signal from the boy the dog moved in a wide circle to outflank the sheep. Then he closed in, yelping his authority. At once the thick-fleeced ewes shifted to his commands and he, running to this side and to that, now cleverly worked them into a group. As Areon led this main group homewards Teg doubled back to round up any stragglers still grazing on the hillside. This was a dog on which he knew he could rely.

By the time he arrived back with the flock Andraemon had completed the pens; and the sheep, harried by the tireless dog, willingly took refuge in them. They counted them: there were thirty six in all. Andraemon reckoned that two were missing. "But the most important thing now is to have your hut made," he said, and scarcely pausing for breath began trimming off some long sticks he had gathered for this purpose.

Areon felt so hot and tired. He mopped the sweat from his brow and looked again to the skies. The sun was no longer climbing. The wind was freshening from the west. High, high above, seagulls were tracing invisible paths towards the mainland. His thoughts turned to Troy: *"About now the trumpets are sounding from the Temple roof. And the people will be strolling home from the shops and work places. Father and Mother are washing and changing before going to sit at Priam's table in the great hall."* He thought of his two brothers and smiled. *"Idaeus and Dolon will be late as always – Idaeus, probably skylarking still with the girls and boys down by the fountain, – Dolon, javelin-throwing as usual."*

The hut was made: Andraemon had done the best he could do. It was getting late and time for him to be returning home. But first he and Areon sat down and shared food together. Neither was Teg forgotten, but was rewarded for his labours with a handsome bone.

Before he left, Andraemon advised him:

"You will be lonely here for a day or two but you will soon get used to it. Keep a watchful eye on your flock all the time for you never know when Calchas or his men may come. There are plenty of rocks lying about: build new pens as soon as you can. Let me see, is there anything else?... Now, you know the way home. Slip back to us on the fifth evening. You may stay overnight with your friends – no one need know about it," he said with a wink of his eye.

"Thank you, Andraemon."

"Farewell, my friend," said the swineherd, and he led his mule away.

For a long time Areon stood there watching him as he walked away growing smaller in the distance. At the brow of the hill the swineherd turned and waved. Then he was gone from view.

Areon was on his own now.

The crimson sun was fast westering as shadows lengthened in the valley. The wind was beginning to sigh and clouds were mustering over the darkening hills. He felt his stomach tighten. Although exhausted, he wanted to be kept busy. Inside the tiny hut he arranged and re-arranged the things Andraemon had left him: a sheepskin, a blanket, a cloak; two bowls and a small stone lamp; the bread and meat, the cheese and a goatskin filled with milk; and the small axe which he placed next to his own adze.

It took him some time to light the lamp. In Troy there were servants to do this for him. Then he sat down, picked up Andraemon's axe and examined it carefully, caringly, in just the same way he knew old Antenor would. He wondered what the carpenter might say if he held this tool in his weathered hands. "A fine bronze axe," he would say, "with a smooth haft of olive.

Yes, a fine piece of workmanship. Always aim for true workmanship, my boy."

Yet when he stepped outside to check the pens again, he held the axe as a weapon, not a tool. Twilight had faded: darkness had descended: no moon or twinkling star brightened the face of the night. He stood at the hut and listened. A ceaseless murmuring rose from the stream beyond. Out in the black emptiness the wind rustled loudly in the trees. He strode uneasily forward. Even in the pitch blackness he felt strangely visible, as if someone or some thing was eyeing him, watching his every move. He stumbled, almost fell, at the pens. Peering inside, he saw the dim animal shapes huddled together, ghostly, silent and still. Hurrying back to the hut he felt the first cold drop of rain on his cheek.

He tossed and turned as he tried to settle himself down for the night. Sleep did not come easily. Outside, the wind soughed and the rain pattered endlessly in mournful rhythm. He tried to think of his homeland again: Troy, in the clear blue light of day: her lofty walls and mighty towers; her paved streets he loved so well; the bright palace where he lived; and the places where he played – the Two Hundred Steps, the Garden of the Sun, and the Potter's Field; the well, the olive grove, the timber-yard, the stables...

But sleep did not come easily. And when at last he found rest a chill wind blew through his dream. In his dream he walked through a wasteland of scorched fields that stretched out, one after the other, to a horizon ablaze... from the fields on his left there rose up the pitiful cries of abandoned beasts... from those on his right sounded the metallic cackling of birds... he started to run, and run and run...

He awoke, his heart pounding. His lamp had gone out. But the streaks of grey light edging the doorway assured him of dawn's approach. He lay back and dozed for a while.

When he woke again he decided to rise. Reaching for his sandals, he noticed Teg curled up in the corner. The little dog peeped up at him and wagged his tail nervously once or twice, for Andraemon always kept him outdoors and only the wind and the rain had driven him inside. Areon smiled and patted him on the head.

"You are welcome here little fellow," he told him. "Even hardy dogs like you must sometimes take shelter. Come along, I'll fetch us something to eat. We have much to do this morning."

Happily sensing that he would not have to sleep out in the cold ever again, Teg sprang to his new master.

Chapter 8

Nesa and Osban were brought by the soldiers to the grain fields where the reapers were already at work. A foreman was waiting for them. His orders were clear and simple:

"You will report here for the rest of the harvest. You will work here from dawn till dusk. One short rest is permitted each day. As soon as the harvest is gathered in, you will be given other duties. Am I understood?"

He was understood well enough. "I don't like the sound of this," said Osban under his breath as he followed the foreman through the field.

All around them the scene was a battlefield of activity. Straight away they were in the thick of it.

With sharpened sickles the reapers advanced, like a band of warriors, cutting a swathe through the massed ranks of corn. As the grain fell away in rows, down swooped the sheaf-binders to snatch it, twist it and tie it with straw. Hanging on the rear came the Trojan pair, detailed to mop up any stragglers that still lay in the furrows. The advance was relentless. No rest was taken, no quarter given.

How they survived that first day in the fields they would never know. In order to keep pace with the sheaf-binders they had to run hither and thither, gathering corn as fast as they could. They were soon soaked in sweat. Soon, also, their arms and legs began to ache and every muscle of their backs groaned under the strain. Any failure to keep up with the advancing troops was met with a volley of jeers:

"What's happening to you?" –

"Look at them: like a pair of headless chickens!"–

"Have you ever worked a day in your lives?" –

"Trojan laggards!"

Yet bravely they laboured on. The sun had reached its highest when at last the foreman called for rest. For Nesa and Osban the relief was enormous, if only temporary. They lay down in the shade, completely drained, feeling light-headed and giddy.

"I can't take much more of this, Nesa," said Osban, meaning every word of it.

"Sure what's a little bit of hard work to a tough one like you?" replied Nesa, and they both laughed despite themselves. She opened the small parcel of food Andraemon had given her. "Here, eat this before you waste away completely," she said, handing him some bread and cheese.

"I'd even prefer that awful sailing ship to this," he said.

"I know. This is like slavery," said she and they laughed again.

"Even that horrible captain and his sailors," continued Osban, "were a good sight better than these witless buffoons."

"I don't know about that."

However, to their genuine surprise, a while later one of the brawny workers came over and offered them milk from a goatskin. The offer was gratefully accepted. They drank their fill, slaking their thirst.

"That was good, I might have to take back what I said about them," said Osban.

Nesa sat up. "Well, look at them, Osban. Have you ever seen anyone in Troy as poorly dressed as these? Have you ever seen anyone made to work as hard? Look at the way that foreman treats them, the way he speaks to them. It's they are the slaves, not us. I pity–" Her words were interrupted just then by the loud voice of that same man:

"Put away your food. Pick up your sickles and get back to work!" he roared.

"Oh, be quiet," murmured Osban, wearily pulling himself off the ground.

So they trudged out to the shimmering field once more. No day would ever again be as long or as hard as this, they told each other.

Mercifully, the day finally came to a close. Reaper and sheaf binder took the road northwards and homewards. Nesa and Osban shambled off in the opposite direction. Never did a road seem as long or as winding as that which led back to Andraemon's homestead that evening. The one consolation was that the good swineherd was there to welcome them, with a cheerful fire blazing and spicy stew simmering in the pot. They were so tired, however, that no sooner had they eaten than they curled up before the fire and fell asleep.

After a while Andraemon tried to wake them but they were dead to the world. He stood looking down with pity upon them. *They remind me so well of the pair I left behind, my own Hushan and Timna. But they at least had their mother to tend to them. These waifs have no one. No one, except me, that is,"* he thought to himself. *"Tomorrow I must let them take the mule with them – it'll be easier on them."* Then lifting them gently – even then they did not wake – he carried them to their little hut and covered them with blankets for the night.

They struggled on with this work for the next number of days. However, no day was to be as hard or as desperate as that first awful day in the fields. Gradually their bodies were hardening, becoming attuned to the tough physical labour. Any jibes thrown about by the workers were now largely good-natured, or "half-witted" as Osban described them.

On a number of occasions the island children joined the workers in the fields. The two Trojans always looked forward to this because it allowed them to slacken off for a while and work at their ease, especially when the foreman was absent. At first the local children were reluctant to talk to the foreign slaves but presently the barriers began to melt and before long Nesa and Osban were accepted as one of their own.

In particular they got to know well the daughter and son of Telemus the reaper, the one who had offered them the milk on that first day. Pero, the lively one, was the same age as Nesa. The quieter one, Nestor, was a year younger than Osban. The pair of them would always come earlier than the rest and stay longer so that they could be with Nesa and Osban. Sometimes they brought food with them which they shared with their new friends.

"Osban, tell me about Troy and all about the war," Nestor would ask each and every morning, until in the end Osban had to invent all kinds of heroic adventures to satisfy his eager listener. Making up wild stories was something he was very good at doing. Pero and Nesa had also struck up a firm friendship – enough for the Trojan to allow the Achaean a glimpse of the amber necklace she so treasured.

It was Nestor who rushed across the fields to them one morning with the warning: "Osban, Nesa, the King's man comes! He rides towards us, look!"

"Quick, make yourselves look busy," called Pero.

They leapt to their feet. The harvesting had almost finished; the past few days had seen them toiling less and less, sometimes even daring – as now – to retreat into the shade for a little chat.

"Where is he?" asked Osban.

"Over there, it's Calchas, I see him," said Nesa.

A two-horsed chariot drove leisurely out from behind the clump of olives at the top corner of the field and turned towards them: Calchas had come to inspect the work on behalf of the King. The foreman was riding the horse beside him.

"My father does not like the King's man," said Nestor in a low voice.

"That makes two of us," muttered Osban.

"He says that whenever he comes we are made to work harder and longer, and we receive less for it. He is a mean man," said Pero.

"I hope he sails away again soon and never comes back," said Nestor.

Every reaper and sheaf binder was bent low once more and hard at work as the two approached. Not to be outdone, the four young people were busier than bees, and quieter than mice, as they gleaned the corn behind. They were all eyes and ears, nevertheless.

Calchas looked pale, drawn and irritable. He had had another bad night's sleep: his back was bothering him again. That recent voyage had done it no good, he remarked to himself. Nor was this bumpy chariot-ride helping much either. He would prefer, simply, to be back in his comfortable office in his comfortable chair among his scrolls and clay tablets. Having to inspect these peasants irked him greatly.

"The work is adequate, I suppose," he told the foreman after a long – and for the foreman, tense – silence.

"My thanks, your lordship."

"Barely adequate, I should say, so don't thank me, man."

"Yes, lordship."

Calchas halted close by. He looked in their direction. "Those two slaves. Any problems?" he inquired.

"None, lordship."

"Well, there is no need for them here any longer. Send them to the palace first thing tomorrow morning. You may have the use of them again for the harvesting of fruit, and later for the olives."

The foreman nodded. The pair of them rode off. Nesa and Osban looked at each other. Both shrugged as if to say: "what's in store for us next?"

They did not have to wait long to find out.

Sunrise saw them drive the mulecart up through the town that sprawled at the foot of the fortress. Its little streets were shadowy and empty. Not a soul yet stirred within its mud-bricked homes. Nesa was not impressed by what she saw: the rude, unkempt dwellings; the streets dirty and unpaved, with not a single statue or flower or light-giving fountain to be seen; the absence of any colour or form or elegance to the place. *This town is about as ugly as Troy is beautiful,* she thought to herself.

Neither of them had a word to say as they drove onwards and upwards, the mule straining against the steep incline.

A shudder of apprehension gripped them as they came before the mighty Gate. One glance to the left and the right at the lions of stone that stood there on guard, the Gate opened, and they entered. They found themselves in a deserted courtyard. Climbing from the cart, they stood and waited. With a sudden clang the Gate closed behind. Turning, Nesa saw the soldiers – a pair at the Gate, four more in the Tower above.

"So this is the lion's den," she muttered within. Then she and Osban drew close together as if to seek one another's protection.

"I don't like the look of this place at all," she heard Osban whisper in her ear.

Presently a middle-aged woman appeared, a servant at least, or a slave, judging by her dress which was poor and without colour. She did not introduce herself, but merely beckoned them to follow. As they entered the wide porch she turned to them, and putting a work-worn finger to her lips, said: "You must tread quietly. No one inside has yet risen." Then she led them through a square-shaped room of brightly painted walls, of reds and greens, yellows and blues. Then, gently pushing open the solid oak doors she brought them into the big hall, the feasting room of King Terpius. The room was garlanded with roses. The aroma of rich food still hung in the air.

"Wait here. I shall return in one moment," said the woman and she left by the small side door.

Nesa gazed about her. Stately columns ran this side and that, supporting a broad ceiling, the centre of which opened into the viewing gallery above. Many chairs were ranged along tables spread with fine crimson covers on which the remains of food were scattered amid baskets, mixing bowls and goblets. Her eye was drawn to the table at the top of the hall, to its large chair, silver-studded and inlaid of ivory: the seat of the King.

"This room reminds me in a way of Priam's Hall at home," she whispered.

"I would not know, I've never been invited," said Osban gloomily.

"Though this place is smaller, darker and nowhere near as grand," she added.

Osban examined the walls which were covered in paintings. He would soon be familiar with the scenes they depicted. On one wall, a woman waves farewell to a long line of foot soldiers as they march to war. On the wall opposite, a party of hunters and their baying hounds surround and kill a dark-maned lion. Another wall shows a pair of hunters emerging from woods: a great-antlered stag is the prize they bear. The final scene shows a dark galley – it carries its warriors homewards across a wind-swept sea.

"I'd like to tear down every one of them," he remarked.

"Now, now, don't speak like that," said Nesa. "You're looking at the work of an artist. You can't imagine how much time and effort went into those."

"Yes, but done by Achaean hands," he replied bitterly.

"Maybe. They are quite good, nevertheless."

"I see nothing in them."

Nesa heard a door opening down the corridor. "Listen, I hear her coming."

The woman entered. She brought with her a broom of willow twigs, some cloths and an old pan. She told them:

"Each morning, this hall must be swept and cleaned." Then she pointed to the hearth in the centre of the room. "Those ashes must be cleared away." Then to the long row of tables: "These must be cleaned and polished." She stepped across the floor and with a sweep of the hand said: "Everything must be left spotless, the tables, the chairs, the floor. And you must polish these," she said, indicating the pair of golden statues in the corner. They were of boys holding aloft their flaming torches. "After that I am told you are to go and fetch the water, and after that to the forest for firewood…"

Osban sighed after she left them: "I can see that this is not going to be any easier than working in the fields."

"Areon does not know how lucky he is, up there in those hills all day with nothing to do and nobody breathing down his neck," said Nesa.

"I do not think he would agree with that somehow," said Osban.

Chapter 9

The moon waxed, the moon waned, month followed on month; summer drifted into autumn; days shortened, trees lost their leaves and the restless swallows departed. Yet all of Nature's ever-changing beauty – the after-glow of an autumn sunset or the trembling of a golden leaf on a bough – passed the Trojans unnoticed. Caught up as they were in the humdrum life of the slave, day crept after day in dread order, each one the same as that which went before or came after. From dawn to dusk they toiled thanklessly for their masters. Soon Areon's sandals were worn, Osban's clothes were dirty and threadbare, Nesa's once soft hands had become calloused and tough.

Now winter had come. The sun was shining weakly out of a pale sky. It was cold.

Areon was out walking on the hill as was his custom each morning after he had released the sheep and completed his camp chores. He moved briskly to keep warm, a big cloak wrapped tightly about him. At the top of the hill he did not pause as usual to survey the island and the outstretched sea but pressed on along the ridge, bracing himself against the uprising wind.

He was thinking of his friends whom he would be meeting later that day. There was so much he wanted to tell them. It was so lonely being on his own all the time.

He had reached the end of the ridge and was on the point of turning back down the valley when something caught his eye. Ships. *"How did I not spot them until now?"* he wondered.

There were at least seven of them, approaching from the south in a direct line towards him. Could they be Trojan? – for one fleeting instant his heart leapt. But hope quickly vanished when he identified them as Achaean – Achaean warships.

With sails furled they ploughed through the sea, close enough for him to see the banks of oars threshing the waters. Feeling exposed to view as they drew closer, he crouched behind a boulder. Now he could make out the figures of the men on board: each ship was packed with warriors. He knew who they were and he knew from where they had come. Even before the welcoming hornblasts sounded over the hills behind, he had begun to suspect the worst. Abruptly, though, he checked these thoughts:

"No, no it cannot be," he said aloud.

*　　*　　*　　*　　*　　*　　*　　*　　*　　*　　*

Word that the men had returned from Troy swept through the palace. Calchas at once ran to tell the King. Soldiers abandoned their posts on the wall and hurried down the steps. In the courtyard, the potters silenced their wheels, stonemasons dropped their hammers and weavers left their looms on hearing the news. Inside the palace, the nobles rushed about excitedly; servants put their work aside; all went outside to join the throng. There was both hope and doubt on every lip and in every heart.

"Could it be just another rumour?" asked one.

"No, it is true, believe me. They have returned," said another.

Nesa, who had been preparing food in the kitchen, slipped out after the crowd into the courtyard. Everyone stood waiting for King Terpius.

At last the old man appeared at the doorway, with Calchas at his side. White-haired, frail, dressed in a robe of purple, he walked with faltering steps to the chariot which awaited him. As he stepped up to his four black horses and to the golden carriage they drew, a change seemed to come over him – a fresh vigour was suddenly restored to his limbs – and he mounted it without assistance. With one wave of his hand he silenced the crowd. His voice was commanding and clear:

"My loyal people, today is a proud, proud day for us. This day above all other days we will remember always… Ten long years we have waited; finally Zeus has granted our dearest wish. The war is over! Our sons return! Let us go forward to embrace them!"

A great roar greeted his words. Unable to contain their joy the crowds immediately surged out through the Gate and swept down towards the harbour. Behind them rode the King's chariot, followed by those of his nobles.

Nesa hesitated a moment. Then, plucking up her courage, she walked out after them. The news of the ships' return filled her with dread. Yet for better or worse she simply had to find out what their arrival meant, for her, for Areon and Osban, for her beloved Troy.

By the time she reached the harbour the ships had rounded the headland and one had already turned into the channel ahead of the rest. An enormous crowd was there to greet them – they stood shoulder to shoulder on the pier – hundreds more were gathered along the muddy shoreline. Unnoticed, she edged her way forward to the mooring place for a better view.

There was an outpouring of great joy as the first ship entered the harbour. All in a dizzy moment the anchor was cast, the ropes were made fast and the long lost men stepped out from the ship. Some wept freely. Some fell to their knees in thanksgiving. Others called out to their loved ones in the milling crowd. Even Nesa could not remain unmoved by the sight of so many returning to the arms of those who had waited so long.

One by one the other ships came in. As the final vessel turned into the harbour all eyes beheld the stocky figure of the commander standing at the bow. The King, who had been saluting the warriors from his chariot, now alighted. He walked to the edge of the pier. He stood there with hands outstretched, his eyes wet with tears. The commander raised his sword to the King: it flashed in the sunlight. But it was the leather helmet he wore which caught Nesa's eye: the helmet rimmed with the gleaming tusks of wild boar.

Closer, closer drew the red bow of his ship. Closer, closer drew the people round their king. All became quiet, only the wind sounded, and the screeching of a lone gull. All were still, the only movement was of the waves lapping fitfully around the pier. Nesa took one look at the commander's face and shivered. It was him.

With one voice the crowd sang out its triumphant greeting:

"Hail Megnor, son of Terpius! Hail Megnor, Warrior Lord! Hail Megnor, Sacker of Troy!"

*   *   *   *   *   *   *   *   *   *   *

The sound of cheering was clearly heard by Osban who was out collecting firewood. He realised some important event was afoot, but continued with his work. This at least was a job he liked doing. Here in the woods he could escape for a while the drudgery of the palace, the feeling of being hemmed in, of being watched over, of having to be constantly on guard. Sometimes, if he and

Nesa worked quickly enough, they even had time to play about for a while – to chase one another, or climb tress, or pick berries.

Nesa, however was not with him today and he had little desire to linger very long. Besides, he was getting curious as to what all the fuss and excitement was about. As soon as he had the wood loaded, he heaved himself up on the cart and made for the palace.

There was nobody to be seen on the normally busy road and in the town not a soul stirred. Arriving at the palace he found the Gate wide-open, the walls unguarded and the courtyard deserted. He drove the mule around to the side and tied it to a post. Then he entered through the servants' door. Everything was strangely quiet. *"It must be something very important, whatever it is. I expect Nesa will tell me all about it when I see her,"* he thought to himself.

He strolled around. There was not a single person about. He went into the kitchen, looking for Nesa: she was not there. What he found instead were the trays of food prepared for the King and his guests: fruits, fish, spiced meats, cheeses, bread made from fine wheat flour, a basket of figs and three dishes of honey cakes. *"Well, now, this is interesting,"* he spoke to himself. *"All this tasty food with nobody here to sample it but you – you who have been working up an appetite all morning. No one would mind, I'm sure, if you nibbled a piece or two!"*

But first he thought he'd better make absolutely sure it was safe to do so. He checked the corridor outside – it was empty. Then he peeped into the storeroom where the great jars of olive oil were kept, and then into the accounts' room next door where Calchas kept his rows of neatly-stacked clay tablets. The way was clear. Rubbing his hands with glee and chuckling to himself, he tiptoed back into the kitchen. He tasted some of the meat first. Delicious. Next he helped himself to some fish – sturgeon, he thought – and then to more meat, and bread. *"It's not wise to be too greedy. One or two little cakes and that will be enough,"* he warned himself.

Just as he was lifting the cake to his lips he heard a sudden clamour in the courtyard. The cake leapt from his hands in his fright. But he composed himself, with a whisper within: *"Stay calm. Do not panic. There is plenty of time."*

He picked up the cake and slipped it inside his tunic. Before going outside he snatched two more, one for each of his friends.

Out in the courtyard he could not believe what he saw. Columns of soldiers came marching in, carried along on a triumphant wave of shouting and cheering. Held high were the spoils of war: jars of stone; bronze jugs and bowls; statues of silver, gold and of ivory; the finest of cloths and rugs; shields, helmets, spears, swords and daggers; and all the many other things he instantly recognised as Trojan. He just stood, dumbfounded.

They piled them in the middle of the courtyard and gathered round in a wide circle. Into the centre rode the chariot of the King, his son, Megnor, at his side. Recognising him, Osban turned and looked away.

All eyes gazed in wonder at the Sacker of Troy and the magnificent prize he held: 'Echelune,' the Sword of Kings, the most sacred symbol of Troy itself. How they marvelled at its blade of imperishable metal and its golden hilt set with twinkling jewels – never before had they seen, or would they see again, a sword as superbly crafted as this. Megnor had indeed brought home a worthy trophy, everyone agreed.

Frozen in that awful moment, the young Trojan wished the ground would open and swallow him up. Vainly, he looked around for Nesa. Where was she? Where was she?

Chapter 10

Later that evening Areon came down the twilit path through the pines to the homestead. The visit was always something he looked forward to so much. This time, however, his heart was fluttering nervously.

As usual a bright fire was crackling in the yard, and Andraemon was still at the sties tending the pigs. Spotting his old master, Teg yelped happily and rushed to him.

"Good dog, good boy, keep the paws down," laughed Andraemon, patting the excited dog. "And how is the young shepherd faring on the hills these days?" he called in greeting to Areon.

"Fine," replied Areon. "It has got a little cold though."

"Yes, I must remember to give you another blanket to bring back with you... Teg! go on, move off with you," ordered the swineherd. His feet were at this moment being licked by the faithful dog. He gave Areon a curious sort of look. "I expect you saw those ships earlier this morning?"

"I did. Have you learned anything of them?" asked Areon nonchalantly.

"Well, I've not spoken yet to anybody who has been to the harbour but I can tell you those ships have returned from Troy."

"I thought as much." Areon was doing his best to hide his concern.

"I wonder what news they will bring to you... perhaps you ought to prepare yourself for the worst?"

"I don't think it will be all that bad," Areon replied; he simply would not, could not, let himself believe otherwise.

"We'll hear soon enough, I suppose, when your two friends arrive. In the meantime let's get things in order around here," said Andraemon, cheerfully rubbing his hands. "There's some fish over there by the fire – caught them myself this morning – fine big ones – would you roast them for us, Areon? I've one or two things still to do."

Areon nodded eagerly. He was tired, hungry and cold; anxious to get to rest, food and the warmth of the fire as quickly as possible.

Andraemon strolled away, disappearing into the dark. The young Trojan threw some logs on the fire, then prepared the fish and spitted them. At last he could sit down. Teg came and lay beside him. Darkness gathered; the fire blazed; the fish roasted.

Had he woken from his brooding thoughts, Areon might have noticed the sky above him slowly fill with twinkling stars. He did, however, hear the sound of cartwheels at a distance. He sprang to his feet and ran to open the courtyard gate. His two friends came riding out of the darkness. Almost at once he caught that terrible frozen look on their faces. He smiled and waved but they scarcely returned his greeting. They drove past him across the yard.

Anxiously he walked back to the fire. He turned the fish and settled back into his seat of brushwood to wait for them.

Before long the two glum figures appeared and sat down next to him.

"Well? What's wrong?" he immediately asked. "You both look as if you've seen a ghost."

There was a long silence.

At last Nesa spoke, her voice scarcely above a whisper: "The city has been destroyed."

"Impossible. That cannot be."

"Everything plundered... our people put to the sword..."

"No, you are wrong. This is wrong! Troy is unbreakable, you know that yourself." He looked from one to the other, almost pleading with them. "Year after year they have tried to break us – they were only wasting their time – not even the gods could throw down the walls of Troy!"

"What she says is true. We've seen it with our own eyes," said Osban.

"Seen what? What have you seen exactly?"

"The ships. The soldiers. The wild boar, Megnor. Remember him? He's back."

"So?"

"Wake up, Areon," said Nesa. "I've seen them unload our treasures off their ships. They have made a huge pile of them in the palace yard. There is no point in denying it–"

"Can you not see what this is?" he interrupted angrily. "They had to come back with something to show after all their trouble, didn't they? Their pride would never let them admit that they had wasted ten years and not won the war!"

"Something awful has happened," said Osban, who had a hunted, haunted look on his face. "I know in my heart something awful has happened... Megnor had Priam's sword in his hand, I'm sure of it."

Areon looked his friend in the eye. "You could not be sure of such a thing, Osban."

"I am. I am, I tell you."

"Even if it is the Sword, that doesn't mean anything. That does not mean Troy is lying in ruins, now does it?"

"No, but it looks bad, very bad," answered Nesa.

He turned to her defiantly. "You saw the ships arrive. Tell me: were any Trojans on board? – slaves, I mean. Have any Trojans stepped from their fine ships? Have you seen any?"

"No. None."

"Well then?"

"They are boasting of how they let no prisoners be taken," she added flatly.

Areon was having none of this. "Yes, they would say that, wouldn't they? Now, tell me: are they boasting also of how they captured the city itself? That will be some tall tale I'm sure."

"I've heard them talk of it, yes," said Nesa.

"Go on, tell me then. I'll not believe a word of it though," said he dismissively.

Nesa sounded so tired now as she began:

"They played a cunning trick on our people... They pretended to give up the siege, and they boarded their ships... It seemed like they intended to set sail for home. But no. They withdrew their fleet behind the island of Tenedos and waited. Behind them on the shore they left a huge wooden horse – an offering to the gods, it appeared. But in the belly of the horse some soldiers were cleverly hidden. When our people came upon it, they suspected nothing and brought it back to the city in triumph. During the night, the Achaeans stole out and opened the Scaean Gate to their army. That is how it happened, how it ended."

"A wooden horse!" Areon laughed. "It all sounds a bit far-fetched, I must say."

"Anyhow, that is what is being said," added Nesa.

"Maybe Areon is right. Things may not be as bad as they appear," said Osban; he was beginning to take comfort from the sheer power of Areon's denial.

"All right. Let us not talk any more of this," insisted Nesa. She knew how stubborn Areon could be once his mind was fixed on something. Besides, there was nothing to be gained by pursuing the matter. "From this moment on we must think, plan and talk about how we are going to escape from this island. That is what we must do."

"Yes," agreed Areon.

"Now you're talking," nodded Osban, his face brightening for the first time.

"No matter what has happened at Troy, whether it has fallen or not, there is no sense now in our waiting here and just hoping to be rescued. Are we agreed about this?" she asked.

"Agreed," answered both in one voice.

"Good. Let us eat then," said Nesa, though in truth she felt little appetite for it.

Chapter 11

Though she had told her friends otherwise, Nesa never really believed that a ransom would be paid for them and that they would be shipped back to Troy. It just seemed like the right thing to say at the time. That was then; this was now. The only real hope of escape, she figured, was to slip away in one of the small fishing boats from the harbour. It would be difficult and dangerous to do this, but with the right planning and a little luck she believed they could succeed.

On a number of occasions over the past few months she had been down to the harbour area with messages and deliveries from the palace. Secretly, she had used these visits to explore the possibilities of escape. As she later told Osban:

"The way I see it, there are three big problems to overcome…"

"Go on, I'm listening," said Osban.

"First, they seem to have put a permanent guard on the harbour. I don't know how we are going to deal with that."

"What about at night? – maybe it's not guarded then."

"Hopefully, yes. We will have to pay a visit there to find out," replied Nesa. "Another problem, a major problem, is that the fishermen always take their mast, sail and tackling away with them each evening."

"But that scuppers everything. How are we to sail away in one of their boats then?"

"I'm coming to that, be patient… The other thing, of course, is that a good clear headstart will have to be made. Timing will be crucial. If the Achaean learns of our escape too soon he will catch us up in his long ship with little difficulty."

"We'd be rightly in the soup then," smiled Osban.

"Don't even think about it!"

"So, tell me, what is your plan?"

"It's very simple, it's like this," said Nesa. "One, we make the sail, oars, mast, ropes, everything ourselves. Two, we escape under cover of darkness on one of the Festival nights when the Achaeans' alertness will be dulled by wine and merrymaking."

"Sounds fairly straightforward, except for number one. Seriously, Nesa, how can we possibly make all those oars and things?" asked Osban.

"This is where we need Areon. Surely he must have learned something useful from that carpenter – heaven knows, he's spent enough time with him."

"That is true enough."

"He will make the oars and the mast. The sails and the ropes, I'm sure we could put together ourselves."

"Or maybe pinch some?"

"You'd like that wouldn't you, you rascal."

"Areon already has the adze and the axe, and I know where to get him a nice little saw," beamed Osban mischievously.

"Good. But be very careful, I'm warning you," said Nesa sternly.

They agreed to talk to Areon about the plan at their next meeting. For the time being they thought it better not to let Andraemon know of their intentions.

Less than a month later the Festival of Adonis was held. That was the first time they went to the harbour to spy.

The night was fine, lit by a half-moon in a sky brightly-speckled with stars. Long before dawn, while the owl called and Andraemon still snored, they rose and followed the faintly glimmering road to the palace. When they neared the place where the road forked to the harbour in one direction, to the palace in the other, they turned the mule into a field and tethered it behind some bushes. They then crossed the fields, skirted the hushed marsh and made for the low sand dunes at the water's edge. Big waves were breaking on the shore and they could not resist delaying there for a spell, frolicking about, chasing and in turn being chased by the foaming sea.

But time, like the tide, was fleeting. They had to press on. Like prowling foxes they moved through the dunes, Nesa leading, Osban stepping into the prints she left behind. The torch-lit harbour now loomed up ahead on their right; crouching, they scampered towards it. Next, they were down on hands and knees; then crawling as near as they dared go. Finally they rolled into a hollow, only two hundred paces from their target.

"This is the perfect spot," said Nesa.

"I didn't think this would be much fun – but it is," said Osban gleefully.

"Forget the fun now: this is serious," she told him. And as if to underline her point, an Achaean sentry suddenly stepped into view ahead under the glare of a flaming torch. She raised a finger. "There's number one."

"Two and three," added Osban almost at the same instant, catching sight of the pair at the other end of the pier.

"What did I tell you?" she shrugged.

Before long they had noted the presence of at least seven

guards in or around the harbour. The area, clearly, was being closely watched.

"I think we may as well pack up for the night," said Nesa then.

But they waited another while.

They had counted yet another guard and Osban, unknown to himself, was beginning to nod, when he felt Nesa's hand tugging at his sleeve.

"Down! There's someone coming."

From a distance down the beach came the sounds of singing, of flutes, and the clash of cymbals. A party of late-night revellers was out serenading the stars.

"Don't fret, they won't see us," Nesa assured him.

"What if it's Megnor?" – the thought of it was like a nightmare to Osban.

"It's not. You won't find his sort out singing. Just keep down, everything will be all right."

"And what about our footprints? – in the sand," said he, never so fully awake as now.

"Just keep still and don't worry," she told him. "They'll not notice anything."

The group came within a hundred paces or so of them, but then cut away across the dunes and passed on, through the fields, heading homewards. Soon their fiery torches had vanished into the night.

"Let's go," said Nesa.

"I'm with you," said Osban, yawning.

Dawn's rosy light was glimmering and small birds singing by the time they came back to the mule. The road to the palace lay ahead of them, and a long day of wide-eyed toil.

As time went by, Nesa expected that the guard on the harbour would be reduced. This proved not to be the case, however. She paid two more visits to the harbour that winter and found, if anything, the guard was increased. Lord Megnor, it seemed, beheld the seas with wary eyes, fearing pirate raids on his new-found treasures. Nor did he fully trust his allies on the mainland. Now that the war which had united them against a common enemy was over, there was a real danger that ancient quarrels might be revived and old scores settled. Therefore a constant watch needed to be kept. By early spring Nesa was counting a dozen or more sentries posted at the harbour.

She had other things to worry about. Since Megnor and his warriors had returned, she had detected a change in the islanders' attitude towards herself and Osban. Up to this, the people had been beginning to get used to them, had been coming to accept them – even if it only meant an occasional nod or a half-smile as they passed on the street. Lately, however, she had felt a distinct iciness in the air. In the palace she and Osban were ignored by the other workers. When they went to collect wood they had to suffer the cold stares of the townspeople. As they passed along the street, children began to point at them, or sometimes to jeer or even – on one occasion – to hurl stones at them.

The reason for the bad feeling was clear. Troy had fallen, but not without a bloody struggle. Many an Achaean father, son or brother had not returned home. Of those who had, a large number were badly wounded. The joy of victory had quickly faded. In its place came a sense of mourning and of anger.

Nor was sadness and anger far from Nesa's own heart. She feared for the family she had left behind. Her mother and father, her two younger sisters, and her baby brother – only ten months old when she had last set eyes upon him: what had become of them? Each day the thought kept recurring to her: *"If we escape, if we survive on the high seas, if we succeed in getting home –what will we find?"* To ponder this was almost too difficult to bear.

She had been on the look-out for her two Achaean friends, Pero and Nestor, for some time as she hoped to glean some information from them. She finally came upon them one day as herself and Osban returned to the palace with firewood. They were strolling along by the side of the road and so she offered them a ride on the mulecart to their house, a small mud-bricked dwelling on the edge of town. It gladdened her that they were not reluctant to accept.

Nor were they afraid of talking to her. Nesa was not going to waste the opportunity.

"You must be kept very busy these days, we have not seen you for quite a while," she remarked.

"Yes, my father has much for us to do," said Pero.

"I suppose, with the war over and the men back home again there is a lot for everyone to do."

"There is," chirped little Nestor. "My uncle Thoas is back. He gave me his war shield as a present."

"Aren't you the lucky one! I bet he's told you some great stories about it all."

"Every time he comes to visit he tells me stories, about the battles and everything, and how he captured Troy," said the boy.

"I'm getting a little tired of hearing them – every night," said his sister.

"And he was wounded as well," added Nestor.

"How?" asked Osban, becoming interested.

"In the arm, by an arrow."

"But how? How did it happen?"

"He ran in, and they were letting loose at him from everywhere –"

"He ran into the city you mean?"

"Yes, spears, arrows, javelins, stones – anything they could hurl at you –"

"He's a footsoldier, your uncle, yes?"

"Yes, and they were running everywhere, trying to escape. And one of them turned – he was climbing these big steps up to the palace, Thoas says – and shot an arrow and struck my uncle in the arm, right here!" said Nestor slapping his shoulder with great effect, "But uncle chased him and caught him and cut him down with his sword."

Pero flashed a look at her young brother but he was too carried away on the wings of his story to notice.

"...and we cut them all down, one by one," continued the boy in one breath, "and we captured the palace, and took all the gold and all the silver. And then we knocked the palace down – the whole place – we took it apart stone by stone."

"I see." The response from Nesa was cold.

"Nestor, you are making big stories out of little stories again," his sister told him.

"No I'm not!" came the indignant reply.

"Why don't you tell Nesa and Osban about what happened to you the other day down at the pond? – that's a story I'm sure they'd love to hear," said she, trying to entice him away.

"Oh yes, wait till I tell you..." began the boy.

Nesa was thankful for Pero's thoughtfulness in this, but would have preferred to hear more of what happened at Troy, no matter how grim.

However, when at last they reached the little house Pero herself returned to the matter. As she climbed from the mulecart she turned to her friend and said in a low voice:

"Don't pay too much attention to what Nestor says. All is not as bad as it seems. I've heard it said that almost all of your people escaped unharmed." She turned to go, but Nesa held her by the sleeve:

"How do you know? What did you hear?"

"I've heard a lot of talk. Everything did not go as planned. The attack was supposed to happen at dawn. It didn't. It took place by night. Someone alerted your soldiers, and a pitched battle was fought inside the Scaean Gate, or so my uncle says. Thousands of your people were able to flee through one of the Gates – is it the East Gate? – and many more slipped away through secret tunnels, and scattered into the darkness. That's all I can say," she whispered. "Your city was destroyed. But not your people." With that she left them.

"Thank you, Pero," Nesa called after her.

The news was nowhere as bad as she had imagined in her darker moments. In fact what Pero said had lifted her spirits, restored her hope and strengthened her resolve to escape.

Chapter 12

They had seen little of Megnor since his arrival and they were glad of it. He spent most of his days out hunting deer or training the young men and women or patrolling the seas in his swift warship. Always he returned to the palace late in the evening; he would retire then to the great hall with his friends to feast till the small hours on the finest foods the royal cooks could prepare.

Only once had they encountered him. One afternoon as they returned to the palace with firewood they saw the pair of sentries at the gate suddenly thump their spear butts and stand to attention. Out came Megnor, riding wildly on his black stallion. The horse was Trojan, another of his war prizes; he spurred it viciously as he thundered down towards them. He reined the frightened animal to a halt and looked at them. Osban turned his eyes away. Nesa glanced up at him but calmly kept on driving the little mule. Megnor looked younger without the beard, she noticed; though the eyes – the cold and leering eyes – were unchanged. And as they drove by, they heard again that same hard voice: "It's my young Trojan pups, I see. I expect you are working hard for your keep?"

Nesa made no reply and kept on driving.

"Halt when I tell you!" he loudly commanded.

Nesa pulled in the mule.

"I did not hear your reply?" he snapped at her.

"Yes?" said Nesa calmly.

"I said: I expect you are working hard for your keep?"

"We are."

"Good."

He laughed then, roughly jerked the reins and rode away.

Nesa sighed heavily. "We must stay out of that man's way as much as we can."

"He's nothing but a wild boar," said Osban scornfully, if quietly.

*　　*　　*　　*　　*　　*　　*　　*　　*　　*　　*

Meanwhile, work on the plan was progressing well. Areon was most enthusiastic about it all. Alone in the valley, he had all the time in the world to undertake the work Nesa had set him. He had the necessary tools, thanks to Osban, whose light fingers had lately provided him with a bow-drill, in addition to the saw. First, he had to carefully select a suitable pine tree for the mast.

He scoured the hill-side slopes for this purpose and having finally made his choice, he felled the tree, trimmed it with his axe, and quite expertly smoothed it. The result pleased him; Antenor had taught him well. Not leaving anything to chance, he buried the mast under a pile of leaves, well away from his camp. The next step would be to make a stout pole for the yard-arm. Then this would have to be fitted to the mast – that would be the tricky part. After that he would make the oars.

As for Nesa and Osban, they had been doing their share. Each night in the hut they sat up for a while making the ropes, some by twining brushwood and willow twigs, some by twisting pieces of hide. Nesa wondered whether Andraemon sensed what they were up to. If he did, he certainly did not let them know. Andraemon was smarter than he let on to be, she knew that. But she trusted him.

Providing a sail was not proving as easy. That would have to be stitched together from pieces of cloth, and these were difficult to come by. She had found one suitable piece of cotton in one of the storerooms and had slipped it out of the palace. However, at least five more were needed.

Areon did not have such problems, she felt. His task was not easier, just more straightforward. She could not help resenting a little his 'freedom of the hills' as she called it. True, it might be a bit lonely for him up there at times, but she would trade places any day. There were few occasions on which she and Osban could escape the stifling atmosphere of the palace. *The work in the cornfields when we first arrived, and also the picking of fruit, and then later the beating of the olive trees – that has been our only relief from drudgery,"* she thought to herself.

Therefore she was glad when, late in the spring, another opportunity for work on the king's farmlands presented itself. The purpose this time was to pick out stones for the dry walls on the border of the estate. To make matters even more agreeable, Andraemon had also been sent by Calchas to work there for the few days.

It felt good to be out in the fields, to breathe fresh air again. The sun was growing stronger, the days beginning to stretch. All around the miracle of new life and growth unfolded. On days like these even this prison-island seemed – if one could forget – a half-pleasant place.

On the fourth day, Nesa and Osban were sitting under a fig tree, waiting for Andraemon to return with the mulecart. Three times already that day they had loaded the cart with rocks but they were not tired.

"Do you think I've grown, Nesa?" asked Osban, and he stood up before her.

"You have, come to think of it. You'll be looking down on me soon."

"Good," said Osban with satisfaction. Although he was a year younger than his two friends, it had always irked him that they were so much taller than he.

"And you certainly have lost weight, especially around your tummy," smiled Nesa. "Although if you keep on filching food from the palace, it won't be for long."

"Sure we've hardly eaten a crumb since we came to this place. I don't know what I'd do if it were not for the odd little treat from the King's dish or Lord Shaggybeard's plate!"

"He's shaved off his beard, silly," Nesa laughed. "Seriously though, you'll have to be careful about taking any food."

"Don't worry, I am."

"Yes, but I would not make too much of a habit out of it, if I were you," she warned. Osban had been helping himself regularly from both kitchen and pantry, and she was becoming a little worried by it.

"I won't get caught."

"I'm just giving you a piece of advice, that's all."

"I don't hear you complaining when I give you a nice bit of cake, do I?" said Osban, smiling that mischievous smile of his. "And Areon was not complaining the other night when I handed him all that lovely food."

"No, but he'd still agree with what I'm saying. He wants to get off island as much as I do –"

"As I do."

"Yes. We must not make them suspicious of us, that's all," she persisted.

"All right, I hear you; I know what you're saying."

"Good."

Osban looked down and patted his stomach proudly with his hands. He was pleased with himself. Not only was he growing, but he was becoming trimmer, fitter, stronger. "Nesa," he asked suddenly. "Like to have a race?"

"Where to?"

"To the trees."

"Okay."

"Go!" he yelled without warning, and away he went.

"Come back, you cheat!" she called, rising to her feet. However, she let him have a good headstart before taking up pursuit. She was an excellent runner and could quite easily beat Osban – or Areon for that matter. But that was not what mattered to her. What mattered was the thrill of the chase.

Across the field they went, clearing the half-built stone wall, dashing down the path towards the olive grove. She always liked to wait just until the last moment before catching him. With forty paces to go, she made her move. In a few swift strides she came up close behind. Osban was panting hard, his head rolling from side to side, his arms and legs combining awkwardly. Desperately he struggled to keep his lead, determined not to let her catch him this time. With one final effort he pressed forward and threw himself down at the foot of the tree.

But Nesa had already pulled up. She had glimpsed the shapes of people among the trees watching them.

"Beat you!" Osban gasped, lying flat out on the ground. "Wait till I tell Areon… He won't believe it…"

Nesa did not reply. She stood, looking away, pretending not to have noticed anything.

Then Megnor rode out from the trees, with at least a dozen of the young people stepping behind.

Osban sat up with a start.

"Stand to attention, Trojan," Megnor barked, glaring down at him.

At once Osban leapt to his feet.

The Achaean turned with a mocking grin and addressed his troop. "Look at this, my young soldiers. While you sweat blood, training in the hills, what do you think these Trojans are doing? Resting in the shade and having fun and games! How the Trojans love their fun and games!" Some of them sniggered at this. Others just smiled contemptuously.

Still panting and fidgeting his tunic nervously, Osban kept his eyes on the ground. But Nesa looked calmly at Megnor, and at this group of boys and girls, most of them the same age as herself. There at the back she spotted Pero. Her Achaean friend glanced away quickly when she saw Nesa looking at her.

"I have to say you run well, young girl – for a Trojan, that is," said Megnor and they all sniggered again. "Perhaps we shall see just how good you are? Give me a javelin. We are going to have a proper race." Megnor snatched the weapon from one of the older boys and galloped a distance across the field with it held aloft. He stuck it upright in the ground and returned. "To there and back. I want four volunteers to give the Trojan a race," he announced, pointing at Nesa. Immediately all of them leapt forward, hands in the air calling out to him. Pleased at this

response, Megnor looked round at Nesa and smiled as if to say: "Now, my friend, you are about to be taught a lesson – just like your people were taught a lesson."

Before she knew it she was standing in line with the four picked by Megnor, two boys and two girls. *"If it's a race he wants, it's a race he'll get,"* she said to herself. Quickly she ran an eye over her opponents. There was only one whom she felt she needed to fear – a slim, fit-looking boy, taller than herself. She thought to herself: *"He's the one. I'll stick to his heels."*

She heard Megnor call them to the starting line. She felt her stomach tighten and her heart thump excitedly.

"Go!" – with a piercing roar, Megnor hurled a javelin to the ground and the race began.

The pace was fast, faster than she expected. The tall boy shot into the lead, and Nesa went after him. The race would be between them. *"Stay with him, do not let him gain ground. You must not let him beat you,"* the thought flashed across her mind.

But his stride was long, powerful; he was pulling away from her. Already sensing victory, his friends yelled and cheered.

"Stay with him… Remember Troy." Nesa felt an instant anger rising within her and a fiery vigour kindling her limbs. *"Megnor will eat his words. It's time to show them something."*

She fought back furiously; and the gap between them did not widen any further. Then little by little she began to reel him back. He cleared the wall. She cleared the wall. He made a wide turn at the javelin. She turned sharply.

Now she was pressing him hard. His crowd were no longer cheering so loudly. Scarcely able to look, Osban bit his lip, clenched his fist, silently urging Nesa on.

They approached the wall again. She had almost drawn level.

The boy frantically threw a glance over his shoulder. The mistake was fatal. At once he faltered, stumbled and fell. Nesa swept past.

"Come on, Troy!" roared Osban, unable to contain himself. As Nesa eased home he ran out and hugged her. All around them there was silence.

What happened next Nesa would remember forever. Megnor, who had been sitting on his horse the whole time, suddenly dismounted and whispered in the ear of one of the boys. Nesa could see that he was fuming. His face was expressionless, but there was a look in the eye as black as thunder. When he spoke, his voice was hard, scornful, icy:

"So you've seen the Trojan run. At Troy I saw them run! When we crashed through their Gate, with our keen swords glinting in the moonlight, they ran. Would they stand their ground and fight? No, the cowards ran for their lives and hid like foxes." He strolled over to where the pair of them stood. His gang shuffled behind him. "You, fat boy," he said to Osban with a sneer. "are you a coward like the rest of your people? Will you run also? Or will you stand and fight?"

Poor Osban looked at him with a strange, nervous smile on his face.

"Are you a coward?" Megnor bellowed at him.

"No," came the almost whispered response.

"That's settled then."

"What is settled?" asked Nesa fearlessly; yet fearful of the menace in the air.

But there was nothing she could do. Megnor stood back. A mean, rough-looking boy stepped out before Osban. He took one look at the Trojan and hit him hard in the face. Instantly, like a pack of wolves, the crowd milled around them in a circle, shrieking. Osban was just standing there, with his hands by his side, and that same silly smile on his face. The boy hit him another blow. And another. And Osban stood there defenceless, alone.

Nesa could only look on in horror. The crowd roared with delight when their hero grabbed Osban, tripped him and threw him to the ground. Now he was on top of him, slapping and punching viciously. Tears came streaming down her face. *"It is I who am responsible. How could I have been so stupid?"* – the thought crucified her.

"STOP!" – from behind them came the command. Someone broke through the fevered circle of spectators. Andraemon. There was a fierce anger in his eyes. He stood among them, looking from one to the other. No-one had ever seen the swineherd act like this before: indeed they hardly recognised him, this man, no longer stooped, no longer downcast, no longer tamed.

They flinched before him and drew back, mumbling to one another.

Andraemon turned to Megnor and addressed him with authority:

"You have done enough for today. You will leave this boy and girl alone. Take your followers and go home."

And Megnor did as he was told. And Nesa was amazed.

Later that evening she threw another log on the fire and sat down next to her friend. Except for a small cut on his lower lip Osban bore no mark of the attack. He was still shaken, though. All the way home on the mulecart he had not uttered a word. All evening she had tried to cheer him up, but to no avail. Even the food he had left untouched.

Out of the gathering darkness stepped Andraemon. He came to Osban and gently placed a hand on his shoulder. "Here, my brave friend, take these," he said, offering him two sweet cakes. "Andraemon baked these and kept them for you – for the fine Trojan soldier that you are." Two cakes he also gave Nesa, and sat down beside them.

Osban nibbled at one of the cakes. He looked a little happier now. For the first time he spoke, quietly: "I thank you, Andraemon, for what you did today."

"If it were not for you, I do not know what we would have done," added Nesa. "Megnor was so horrible."

"Megnor… pay no heed to Megnor. I have known him a long time, since before the war," said Andraemon with a sigh. "He was angry and frightened then – both bully and coward – just as he is today. Nothing changes with him. I struggle to understand how that fellow's mind works."

"If he has a mind," said Nesa.

"And if it works," chirped in Osban.

Chapter 13

Early in the fifth month, Areon, as he had been instructed, brought his animals down to the big field outside the town for inspection. Andraemon came with him. Three other shepherds were there as well with their flocks. Islanders and freemen, they were twice his age. They chatted among themselves, eyeing him with curiosity.

Calchas was late as usual. He appeared eventually, riding down in his chariot, his face etched with that look of discontent and disdain with which they were all familiar.

"You stay where you are. I'll look after this," Andraemon told the young Trojan, and he took the flock to the pens at the other end of the field.

Areon stood and waited.

"Almost a year has passed since the day of my capture," he thought to himself. It had been a year of hardship, of loneliness and of pain, yet somehow he had managed to keep a brave face, to keep the chin up as his father used to say. At least now there was some hope. Only the previous day he had completed the oars of fir and hidden them. What he needed was the patience to sit and wait for the signal from Nesa.

"One thing is certain, though: another year – another half-year – will not pass before I return to Troy," he whispered within.

At the bottom of the field the sheep were being inspected, counted and separated: some to be sold, some to be fleeced, some to be butchered. Areon watched uncomfortably as Calchas turned to examine his flock. The inspection did not take long. Then he noticed Calchas beckoning Andraemon to come before him. *"What are they talking about?"* he wondered.

Shortly afterwards the swineherd came shuffling up the field towards him, and Areon's sense of discomfort increased to alarm – even from afar he could tell that something was wrong.

There was no mistaking the look of concern on Andraemon's face. He walked up to the Trojan, placed his hands on his shoulders, looked at him, but said nothing.

"Well?" shrugged Areon.

"Oh, he is pleased. You have looked after the King's flock well – too well, I fear."

"What do you mean?"

Andraemon stepped back from him, grimacing, running his big hands up through his beard and over his face and through his hair and over the top and back of his head. "My young friend, it is the custom on this island–" he paused, "it is the custom on this island at this time of year to separate the sheep, as you can see, and to bring the older ones to higher pastures for the rest of the summer and –" he paused again.

"And I have minded the sheep so well that Calchas wants me for the job?" added Areon.

"Correct."

Areon immediately understood what was meant by higher pastures. He would have to bring the animals to the mountains at the far end of the island, and live alone there, even further away from Nesa and Osban.

"When do I leave?" he asked dejectedly.

"First light, tomorrow," came the reply.

That night he stayed with his friends. He ate little, spoke little. Even Nesa could not dispel his gloom:

"When you think of it, Areon, it's not all that bad," she had tried to assure him. "Everything will go ahead as planned; it will work out. I promise. We can even meet up somewhere – we will have to anyway."

"Where? How?"

"Somewhere in the hills. At your hut maybe. At the next full moon. What do you say?"

"The hut is as good a place as any," he sighed.

At dawn he gathered his animals, both sheep and goats. They made for a noisy, nervous lot and poor Teg, darting to and fro and up and down, found it a difficult task to keep them ordered. He followed the route Andraemon had mapped out for him on a piece of bark. It took him out the south road through the wide plain where most of the island's crops were cultivated. Here, wheat and barley thrived on the fertile soil; orchards, vineyards and olive groves flourished. The fields were empty; a veil of silence hung over the little cottages at the side of the road; it would be some time yet before the farmworkers rose.

When the road finally came to an end, he walked a well-worn track leading to a huddle of wooded hills in the distance. Behind these rose two big mountains, one after the other: the smaller one was smooth-shaped, and green with trees; the second, which rose more steeply, was rugged and ridged, its upper slopes bare and rock-strewn.

By now the animals had quietened and Teg, no longer harassed, was moving at his ease. Areon strolled along and whistled a tune to himself. *"The situation is not so bad,"* he tried to tell himself. *"I have got used to living alone in the valley, and I will get used to this.*" But his stomach, which was churning ceaselessly, spoke more eloquently than his thoughts.

He came to a ravine between the hills where a swift river flowed, choking on sharp rocks. There he let the animals drink their fill while he rested and had something to eat. Then he moved his flock along the bank and on through many twists and turns of the river before crossing and taking a steep path to the top of the hill on his left. Below him now he saw a valley, green and wild, and rising beyond, the broad mountain which hemmed it in.

"All we have to do now is cross that and we're almost there," he said to Teg, who had come up and nuzzled close against his master. He patted the little dog and stroked his ears. "Andraemon was right when he said you were the best. The best dog in the whole world – even if Osban may not agree."

He descended and walked across the valley. *What a fine place for tending sheep,*" he thought, and found it strange that no track of man or beast was to be seen there. Murmuring streams trickled through meadows bright with yellow daisies. Small birds sang in every bush. Over here, willow trees grew, their branches sweeping the ground. Over there, stood towering oaks, with roots old and twisted. *"A nice place; yet there is something about it I do not like,"* he thought to himself.

The further he walked the more this feeling of unease grew. The animals also seemed to sense something, for they slowed, huddled close to one another, fretting about which way to go.

He stopped to listen again. He looked ahead. Forty or so paces away the meadow narrowed into a dark corridor between the bushes and trees. He sensed a danger lurking in that darkness.

"Or am I just imagining it?" he wondered.

Unsure of what to do, he hesitated. At that very instant six or seven deer bounded out from the trees and swept across the meadow in front of him. With that the sheep, and then the goats, turned sharply to the left and broke away in confusion and fear. He hurried after them, relieved that the animals had made his mind up for him. *"For once the shepherd will follow his sheep,"* he said to himself, only too glad to make a detour from the place.

Any feelings of unease were soon forgotten in the hard climb to the top of that mountain. Picking his steps among the rough stones, he slowly wound his way up between the pine trees. His legs ached, he was breathless with the effort. But it was worth it just to survey the new horizons that opened all around, and the ocean so calm and so blue, stretching away to a boundless sky. Areon stood there, alone with himself.

He looked back to the north and caught sight of Megnor's fortress peering out over land and sea. Even at that distance, it seemed too close for comfort. Yet that was where his friends were and he wished he could be closer to them.

Then he descended along the southern ridge of the mountain, turned westwards towards the sea and crossed slopes that were furrowed with lush, well-watered gullies. Thankfully, Andraemon had drawn his map well and he at last found his way to his new home, a cave close to a small, shingly beach.

He was quite pleased with what he found. There was plenty of grass for his hungry flock. Close by, a mountain stream gushed freely down over the stones. The cave was dry, and large enough to house his flock. He could see that it had been used some years previously. Outside it was the remains of a wall which had once closed in a small courtyard. Inside there were pens for the animals; some discarded baskets were lying about; and in the corner he found the ashes of an old fire. Somehow he felt better knowing that another person had lived there before; it made the place feel less lonely, less forgotten.

Unlacing his sandals, he strolled down to the water's edge. Andraemon had given him a line and some hooks, as well as a small net, and he was looking forward to putting them to good use. *"Tomorrow I will catch some fish and roast them for my supper,"* he told himself confidently. The thought of it made him feel hungry. And right now he was hungry, and tired. But there was work yet to be done before he could sit and eat.

Chapter 14

No wonder Osban had resorted to stealing food, for they were never fed in the palace. They were required to work all day long for nothing in return, not even a morsel – it was monstrous. Each evening they returned to the homestead, exhausted and hungry. But Andraemon was good to them. His smile was always welcoming; his fire always blazing; and there was always something tasty in the pot, and plenty of it.

Afterwards the good swineherd would take out his knife and carve on a piece of wood, or make sandals from a piece of oxhide, and they would sit back and talk. They talked of the day they had, they shared stories, sometimes they joked. Listening to Andraemon, they learned much of his homeland, Paddan Aram; and that land and its people soon came to have a special place in their hearts. The earth of Paddan Aram and the sky above it became real and familiar to them. They knew of its valleys and rolling hills, its rivers and streams, its trees, its flowers, its variety of birds and beasts. They heard of its legends and heroes and learned of the ancient ways and customs of its people.

"You must often have thought of escaping from here?" Nesa asked him one evening.

"Many times," he replied, and a shadow passed over his face. "Many times in the past, but no longer."

"Have you ever tried to?" she pressed him further.

"Once, many years ago," he answered quickly. He paused some time before continuing: "There were two others, older men than I. They had been planning to get away for a long time... A runaway has only one means of escape from the island of Leucas: take an Achaean boat, it's as simple and as dangerous as that."

Osban and Nesa exchanged glances at these words.

"We drew lots. Two men, to go for the boat. One man, to wait further down the coast with the provisions – water, food, weapons, that sort of thing... By the will of the Almighty One, I was the one chosen." Andraemon smiled wryly and shook his head. "So I took myself there (not far from where your friend, Areon, is today). I lit a small beacon fire as arranged. I waited and waited. Dawn approached. But no sail appeared. I realized something had gone wrong. I killed the fire and stole back to my hut.

"Pretending nothing was amiss, I took up my work again that morning. I soon heard what I dreaded to hear. My friends had failed and had been captured. I never saw them again. The Achaean does not take too kindly to runaways, you should understand."

Nesa started at the words 'you should understand', and the way Andraemon looked at them. Was he referring to them?

She had no further question to ask. The three of them sat there for another while but there seemed to be little else to say. Presently they retired to bed.

"So much for our escape plan," muttered Osban dejectedly as he pulled his blanket around him.

"Have you any better ideas?" said Nesa with some irritation.

"You have heard what Andraemon said. You have heard what happened to his friends," said Osban.

"What about it?"

"Well, you don't have to be a genius to see that we don't stand much of a chance either, do we?"

If Nesa was downcast by what Andraemon had told them, she did not show it. "I don't know what you are talking about. That was a different situation, different people, a different time. Our plan will not be the same as theirs. We won't take any chances. Of course, it's not going to be easy, I admit that; we are taking a risk. But there is only one way to escape from this place, as Andraemon himself said."

"Could we not cross to the mainland?"

"Out of the question."

"I just hope you know what you are doing, that's all."

"I do. Now turn over and go to sleep," she told him. "And let me not hear you talking like this again."

"Yes, master," he jested.

"Goodnight, Osban."

"Goodnight."

Reassured by her words, Osban was first to drop off to sleep. She lay awake. She envied him who could so easily find rest and who now snored away to his heart's content. She could not cast off her cares so easily, especially with Andraemon's story still echoing in her ears.

She lay there thinking of her plan, examining and considering every part of it. In her mind's eye she pictured the night of the escape, followed every footstep of the path she would take to the harbour, saw the hiding-spot where she would lie in wait, and imagined the awful moments when she would make the move towards the boats – her heart beat fast at the thought of it.

"Will we succeed?" she wondered. *"Yes, why not? But not unless and until that guard on the harbour has been allowed to lapse. There is nothing we can do but wait."*

While Nesa tossed and turned, Osban lay entwined in the soft arms of sleep and dreamed. In his dream he saw again his beloved land; saw himself stride freely along a foaming shore under the pale light of dawn. His head was held high, his hand rested on the hilt of the sword, Echelune, by his side. Faithful Rinja ran to welcome him, and a stallion – black as the night that had passed – stood waiting. Then he rode like fury, and the wind whistled and the golden scabbard clanked; small birds broke out of the grasses in front and the dust rose up behind.

Away to his left he saw the dim fires of herdsmen on the plain. On his right, Mount Ida, crowned with snow, rose out of the mist. And so he came to the edge of the river, the one they call Scamander, and raced along her banks. On and on the waters flowed, and on and on the stallion ran... Then all at once the river faded from his dream. A great and dark forest stood before him, barring his way. He halted and dismounted. He listened. Someone somewhere was calling his name. Was that a drum beating? the sound of trumpets?

The dreamer awoke with a start. It was pitch dark. The wind was blowing hard, rattling the door of the little hut. His eyes were moist and his heart was beating fast.

Chapter 15

Alone in the mountains Areon began to ponder the same questions over and over again. How many days would he spend a slave? How many nights alone? The plan of escape – would it work? When would Nesa ever give the signal? If they were caught, what would be done to them? If they got away, how would they fare on the wild ocean? Would they be able to find a way home? And Troy?... was it true? was it true?

Though haunted by these fears, the flame of hope still burned in his heart. Between hope and despair was a tension, difficult for him to bear. It was worse in the evening, after the day's work was done, when he would sit in the cave, listening to the sound of the sea and to the flickering fire as it softly hissed, throwing shadows on the wall. Then he would think of Troy. Troy, dressed in the beauty of a summer's morning. Troy, so calm and fair – how clear a picture he held of his beloved city! And yet how quickly it dissolved!... Long, long after the fire died, he would sit in the dark and think of home.

Here, he had all the time in the world to himself. There was no one to disturb him, no one to order him about. He could walk the hills or toss stones from the cliffs or search for fish among the rockpools, he was free to do as he pleased.

But he was not free. The chains that bound him were stronger than iron. And as each day passed, he was feeling more and more trapped.

There was a glen in the mountains which he often visited. Good pasture was to be found there and a cool shade among the pines. A stream trickled through the place, filling a pool of crystal-clear water. Beside the pool was a flat rock, his favourite resting spot.

Here, late one afternoon, he sat looking skywards, his feet dangling in the refreshing waters. He was thinking of his friends whom he was to meet again at his old hut in a few day's time.

A hawk – a kestrel, he thought – came suddenly into view skimming over the tops of the trees. Just as suddenly, it halted and hovered in the breeze. As he watched, waiting for it to strike, he thought he heard the sound of a distant commotion. Teg, who was stretched out beside him, immediately cocked an ear and sprang to his feet. Areon lifted his feet from the pool and turned to listen, but the sound had faded away. He sat puzzled for a moment. He looked again for the bird but it was gone.

"What was that all about, Teg?" he asked.

The dog returned a quizzical look, that black patch on his eye somehow always made him look so comical. Areon smiled at him. "Sometimes I think they should have called you 'Patch' instead of 'Teg'... And sometimes I think I must be going mad, talking to you – and what's worse – expecting an answer!"

Just then the sound returned on the wafting breeze and he recognised the baying of hounds. Somewhere in the hills a hunt was in progress.

"I think we shall investigate," said Areon, putting on his sandals.

Teg led the way. The dog knew exactly where he was going, and quickly brought him out through the thick tangle of bushes at the narrow end of the glen and then up and across the bare slopes. During this time no further sound of the hunt could be heard. However, just as they drew near to the top of the ridge there was a burst of baying from the other side. The uproar was sudden, terrible and close. Areon immediately stopped in his tracks, as did Teg. He called the dog and took hold of him. Cautiously, he walked forward. The ferocious baying continued unabated. Teg began to whine, reluctant to press on, and Areon had to coax him to come with him. When he reached the top, he got down on the ground, pulling the dog down with him.

Even before he looked he knew that some animal had been cornered by the bloodthirsty pack. *"A stag more than likely"*, he thought to himself. But what he saw surprised him, shocked him. Some two hundred paces away a huge brown-backed creature suddenly came into view surrounded by its attackers. Areon had to look again before he could believe it:

"A lioness!" he gasped.

She was trapped within a double ring of enemies. The first was of hounds. The second was of men armed with spears and clubs.

He watched as for a while she stood her ground and held them at bay. The hunters and the hunted, it seemed, were frozen in time and space. But then came the moment when the ring about her tightened and the hounds went at her from all sides. One made a run at her from behind, two more rushed in to lunge at her flank. Turning rapidly, she struck the first a blow, then spun around lashing out with tooth and claw. The one hound was felled, the other yelped in pain. The ring of attackers drew back in disarray. Then the lioness roared, roared mightily with a fierce and ancient pride.

She saw her opportunity and grasped at her only chance.

With one bound she broke away, sending dog and man scurrying from her path. She went in behind the bushes and Areon lost sight of her momentarily. Then she appeared again away to the right, with the hounds in hot pursuit. She dodged between some small trees, came out into the open, turned one way and the other, hoping to outwit her tormentors. Altering course again, she came charging up through the undergrowth. With mounting horror Areon now saw that she was coming in a direct line towards him.

But the hounds had her outflanked and she would never reach the ridge where he lay.

In a last desperate attempt to outmanoeuvre them she swerved, her hind legs came from underneath her and she was down. Instantly, they pounced for the kill.

Yet still she fought. Somehow struggling to her feet, she broke free again, only to be brought down again. This time the hounds would not let her away.

Men on horseback came thundering across, weapons upraised. Behind, came the runners, hooting and howling like wild animals. No longer could Areon bear to look. He shrunk back in horror and buried his head in his hands.

He lay there and waited for the death-struggle to take its course. He prayed for the bloodcurdling noise of the hounds to cease, for the cries of the men to fade away. He waited, and it seemed an age passed before silence returned to the hills.

He wanted to walk, to escape, to go somewhere.

But it was down to the place of the kill that his feet brought him. Trampled grass and a few dark red stains were the only reminders of the deed. All was peaceful; all was quiet; the birds were singing again, as if nothing had happened.

And so he moved on down through the valley.

The presence of the lioness on the island puzzled him. Andraemon had assured him that this place was free of such creatures. *She could only have crossed from the mainland – and recently*, Areon reasoned. *She must have been hunted over there, was cornered probably, and she crossed the channel to escape.*

Then his mind went back to that day when he first led his flock through this same valley. He recalled how strangely the animals had behaved, how they had halted, refused to go further, as if sensing a danger here; how they had suddenly broken away from him and scattered in fear. *The lioness must have been there that day, hidden in the bushes,* he figured. He realised that had she lived she would sooner or later have come to visit his flock again, and his sorrow over her death was mingled with a sense of relief.

A sharp yelp from Teg woke him from his thoughts. The dog had suddenly recoiled in fright from something he had come across in the long grass.

"What is it, Teg?" he called out.

Cautiously, he stepped up. His eyes fell upon a small, spotted ball of fur, well camouflaged against the dry grass. Still petrified with fear, the tiny creature lay there, trying to hide its face. Areon's heart went out to the lion cub which looked so helpless, alone and lost.

As he bent down and picked it up gently it gave a little cry of protest. "You poor little creature," he whispered in its ear.

He turned to Teg who was sitting there, looking up with those big puzzled eyes of his. "Come on, boy, let's hurry. This little one must be very hungry by now."

Wasting no time, he gathered the flock and returned to the cave. He sat down, put the lion cub on a blanket beside him and began to milk one of the ewes. Soon he had enough warm milk to fill a goatskin. Gently but firmly, he took the cub up in his arms again. Tenderly, he coaxed it to feed. To his delight it began to take the milk, somewhat reluctantly at first, then more and more hungrily until it had almost emptied the last drop.

"Such a big appetite for a thing so small," said Areon, pleased with his success.

He sat back a while with the cub cradled in his arms. Its hunger satisfied, it seemed no longer afraid, for it lay peacefully, licking its paws, occasionally glancing up at him. In less than no time it was asleep.

Areon stared at the creature in disbelief. A lion, he knew meant only one thing – problems. However, he had no choice but to care for it. His heart, not his head ruled in this matter.

What will Nesa and Osban say when they see it? he wondered. He could hardly wait to see the look on their faces.

Chapter 16

"Have you a name for her?" asked Osban, holding the cub out before him.

"Not yet. I thought of calling her Edro – we once had a cat of that name", said Areon.

"Not Edro, that's terrible," said Nesa. "Why not call her Queen or Kaela – or anything but Edro!"

"Kaela will do just fine, that's what we'll call her," said Osban. He lifted the cub up close to his face, looking into her eyes. "How do you like your name little one? I think it's a perfect name, don't you, a name fit for a queen." The cub licked him on the face as if to say 'yes, thank you, I do like my name'. Osban squealed with delight. "Her tongue feels so strange!"

"It's rough, isn't it, " smiled Areon.

"Rough as gravel," agreed his friend.

"Here, let me hold her for a while," said Nesa, who had been patiently waiting her turn.

Areon was tired after the long walk to the meeting. He had carried the cub the whole way. He had decided to spend the night here in his old hut and wished his friends could stay with him. But they would have to leave soon.

Osban handed over the cub to Nesa. "Will you bring her back to Troy with you, Areon? She'd make a great friend for Rinja." Osban's dog was seldom far from his mind.

"That's what I want to talk about," began Areon. "About getting to Troy."

"She'd gobble up your Rinja in one mouthful," laughed Nesa. "And she'll probably devour every one of your sheep as well, Areon."

"I'll worry about that another time," said Areon. "What I want to know is: when are we going to get away from here?" He looked intently from one to the other, waiting for an answer.

Osban looked at Nesa. She put the cub down beside her, and shrugged. "I don't know," she replied.

"I've got everything ready, the mast and the oars. You've got the ropes and the sail. The boats are in the harbour. Why don't we just take our chance now and escape?" said Areon with a hint of exasperation in his voice.

"It's not as simple as that."

"Why not?"

"Because it is not safe to go yet. You know that as well as I do."

"Well, I'd be prepared to take the risk," said Areon sharply. "We've spent over a full year in this place."

"Listen to me, Areon, if we tried to escape now we'd be caught red-handed, take my word for it. The harbour is still swarming with guards, isn't that so?" she said, glancing at Osban who nodded reluctantly. "We have got to be patient and wait. That is the only way to do it. Myself and Osban are doing our best to keep a watch on the harbour whenever we can. It's not easy on us either."

"I know that. It's just that we can't keep on waiting forever. I can't anyway."

"You'll just have to," said Nesa, her dark eyes flashing. "We will make our move when the time is right, not before. Don't you agree, Osban?"

The pair of them looked at Osban. But he made no reply, only struggled clumsily to his feet and stood before them, grinning from ear to ear. "Forget about all that. I've got a more important question," he told them,giving them that mischievous look of his and at the same time reaching his hand inside his tunic. "The question is, what do you think I have here?"

Nesa and Areon looked at one another in mock surprise. "Don't tell me that he's done it again!" Nesa screeched.

"Yes, I have, I'm afraid," beamed Osban.

"I warned you not to. You are a little rascal."

"Yes but this is a special occasion, Nesa," said Osban, pretending to be serious. "It is not often these days you or I have the honour and pleasure of meeting Areon, our fine friend and fellow-slave, is it?"

"Hurry on and show us what you've got for us there. I'm beginning to feel hungry," said Areon.

"So to mark this occasion, my dear friends," continued Osban, "I would like to present you both with a small gift – a small but sweet gift." With a quick flourish he produced the three cakes. With a flick of his wrist he tossed one to each.

"Well done," cheered Areon.

"You are a true scoundrel," Nesa told him.

They sat close together and ate, savouring each morsel of cake. Teg lay beside them, chewing on the bone Andraemon had sent for him. Nesa had Kaela nestled in her arms, and the cub was soon fast asleep.

"I think she's about a month old," she said after some thought.

"I don't even think she's that old," said Areon.

"She's a month old at least," she insisted. "Do you realise just how big she is going to be in another two months? You may feed her on milk for the time being, but what will you give her then?"

"I don't know," replied Areon.

"Let her loose on the King's sheep!" said Osban with a laugh.

Areon laughed too, but a little nervously.

Chapter 17

Nesa was right about the cub. In the space of two months Kaela doubled in weight and size. Areon was astonished – during that time he had fed her solely on a diet of milk. At first the feeds had to be given at regular intervals but as time went on Kaela was able to take more milk less often. Her teeth had grown also, and it was obvious that they were now big enough for meat eating. The problem of what next to feed her was something Areon began to ponder.

Still, he was delighted to have the cub around. Kaela was a most amusing companion, even if she was always up to all sorts of mischief. Morning was when she was most active. At the break of day, as soon as he released her, she would shoot from the cave like a stone from a sling. Immediately she'd fly head-long for the sea, only to halt abruptly at the water's edge and scramble into retreat as the first wave broke on the shore. This game with the waves would continue for a while, until the sheep and goats appeared. Then the fun would start. In an instant she'd rush to scatter them, then race and chase them for all she was worth. This cat would chase anything that moved. She even chased her own tail – a spectacle that always made Areon laugh. Quite often a pot would be overturned or a pail of milk spilled, but Areon enjoyed the sport too much to mind.

Nor did Teg seem to mind this troublesome stranger who had invaded his territory. Indeed it was touching to see how well the little sheepdog and the cub got along with each other. From the beginning Teg accepted her, allowing her to cuddle up and sleep beside him in his corner of the cave. Teg treated Kaela like a sister, a younger sister, who needed to be watched over.

He was endlessly patient with this cub who was up to every trick, who wanted to play all morning and who followed him everywhere.

Thankfully, Kaela rested for most of the afternoon. She'd disappear under some shady bush and doze peacefully while the blazing sun strained on its high plane. And once she lay down and made herself comfortable she was not willing to shift! "You are such a lazy thing," Areon would say, wagging his finger at her.

Areon gave her a big feed each evening. After that it was time for more fun and games. Kaela loved to stalk, especially at this time of day. Areon and Teg were her favourite targets. Hidden in the long grass, she would crouch and creep towards her unsuspecting victim. She moved ever so slowly, always closing in from behind, her body always kept close to the ground. When she got to within striking distance she would suddenly charge at full speed and pounce. She had outgrown Teg by now and could quite easily throw him to the ground. This she did time and time again, but the little sheepdog, forever good-natured, took it all in the spirit of the game.

"What size will she be in another two to four months?" Areon wondered. He could not continue feeding the lion milk much longer. It was time to do something. "Would she eat fish?" he asked himself. If she did, the problem would be solved. He decided to go and find out.

If Kaela was to be fed on fish, then he'd have to be a more successful fisherman than he had been up to this. Fishing in the cove he had never caught anything bigger than a sprat.

Further down the coast past the cliffs there was a number of small beaches and rocky inlets – he would try his hand there.

Armed with hook, line and sinker, he set out the following evening. He headed across the slopes at a brisk pace, Teg and Kaela following behind. The sky was cloudless and blue, the sea bluer still, both coming together in a hazy horizon. The only sound was the restless murmur of the sea and the "cheer-eet" "cheer-eet" of the swallows on the wing. *"A perfect day for a spot of fishing,"* he thought.

But he was mistaken. If the fish were there, they certainly did not bite. For what seemed like an age he stood on that rock in the water as the white-hot sun turned to gold, grew bigger as it declined, became red and slowly painted the sea the colour of wine. At the end of the day he had not even a sprat to show for his efforts. It was so disappointing. He trudged unhappily back to the cave, yet determined to return the next day.

Return he did, and the following day, and the next. Four days and still nothing on the line. He was moving further along the coast, from cove to cove, swapping one rock for another. He had neither the skill nor the luck of the fisherman, it appeared. However, he had the patience, although even this was beginning to wear a bit thin. But he enjoyed the exploring if not the fishing; went paddling in the crystal waters; threw stones for Teg; held tug-o-wars with Kaela; collected seashells to bring back to the cave.

"Unless I catch something today," he told himself the next evening, *"this will be my final attempt at fishing."* He had come to a small rocky headland at the southwestern tip of the island. Beyond this point he would not venture. Wasting no time, he selected a spot, hooked up the bait and cast out the line. He waited.

Presently two ships appeared from opposite directions, heading towards each other. One was a merchant ship with a crimson sail, striped white. The other was a warship with sail furled, its row of white-painted oars gleaming in the sun. He watched them come closer to each other. Little by little the space between them grew smaller. They met and passed. Then he watched the space between them grow larger again, until they had drawn apart to distant corners of the sea once more. And still the line hung limp and dead in the water. It was a waste of time, he felt.

He decided to call it a day.

Having wound up his line, he climbed to the top of the bank and called the dog and the cub. When they did not appear he had to go looking for them. The sound of Teg's barking led him to a small pebbly beach tucked into the far side of the headland. There was the pair of them chasing each other round a log that had been washed up on the shore. It suddenly struck him that he could use that log to go out to deeper water and fish. If he was successful he could make a canoe or raft for himself. *"Why did I not think of this before?"* he thought. But even before he ran down the gentle slope to the beach, a far more interesting sight caught his eye.

Upturned on the sand, like the skeleton of some strange beast, was the wreck of a fishing boat.

He walked around it, examining it. It must have been lying there for a long time, for its covering of pitch had worn away and its timber was bleached by the sun. Spiders' webs hung from it and tiny creatures had made it their home. All the planks had been ripped from its side, so that only the ribs remained, jutting out like bones from the keel. He walked around it again, touching and feeling, pushing and pulling every part of it. The wood

was good, the structure was strong, he believed. He put one foot against another and counted nineteen feet from stem to stern.

He stood back and looked at it. "Well, this is an interesting discovery," he said out loud. Already his head was beginning to swim with ideas. But there was no time to waste – he wanted to paddle out on that log and drop that line one last time.

With Teg and Kaela running in circles around him, Areon heaved the log down to the water. He threw off his tunic and waded out into the sea, pulling the log with him. The wood was dry and light in the water and floated easily when he climbed upon it. He paddled out cautiously from the shore. Both dog and lion, looking somewhat puzzled, sat on the sand and watched.

Thoughts crowded his mind: *"Maybe I could do something with that wreck? I could rebuild it. We could sail home in it... What would Nesa say? She'd never believe it could be done. She'd want to stay with her own plan. She'd probably be right. I could never repair a boat like that. How could I?... But all it needs is some side-planking, a mast-box and a steering oar. We have the mast, the sail, the oars already. And I have all the tools I need....But I could not work on it where it is – too dangerous. It will have to be moved.*

But how?... I wonder what Osban would think. Nesa would say I'm mad. She'd be right. I'm only dreaming... It could be done, though. I could do it.... I should keep it a secret for the time being... Imagine sailing home to Troy in a boat like that... in my own boat." So he sat astride the log, scarcely aware of the line he had cast into the deep water or of the sun that had become big and red above the quivering line of the ocean.

The sight of Kaela dragging his tunic about shook him from his thoughts. The frisky cub was marching off up the beach with it and Teg was in pursuit. In a moment another tug-o'-war would commence. Just as Areon let a roar at them he felt the line draw tight in his hand. A fish!

He came in with it as fast as he could. It was a big handsome fish, almost half the length of his arm, and its rows of golden scales gleamed in the last rays of the sun.

"Look what Areon's brought you!" he called to the cub.

Dropping the tunic in the sea, Kaela came running towards him. Areon unhooked the fish and threw it to her:

"Here, Kaela, wait till you get a mouthful of this!"

She pounced on it and took it up in her jaws. Almost immediately she dropped it with a look of disgust, as if to say: "This cold thing is horrible. Why did you give it to me?"

Areon laughed at both the cub and himself. "I must have been a fool to think she'd eat a fish."

Back at the cave he sat outside, watching the full moon climb slowly above the mountain, and ate the roasted fish. He was hungry and it tasted delicious.

Without him noticing, the lion came up and stole a piece of the fish from his hand. Areon was surprised and pleased:

"So you've changed your mind about the fish, I see."

He now shared a big helping of his supper with the cub, who swallowed it down hungrily. Areon smiled to himself. *"So she'll eat it cooked! At least that's one problem solved."*

His attention soon turned to the boat. The excitement of the find had not left him. In his mind's eye he saw Antenor, Troy's finest craftsman. He pictured the pair of them walking along the battlements as they used to do, the old man carrying his axe in one hand and boring-tool in the other, and he coming behind with the bag of hardwood pegs. He had learned such a lot from Antenor in the short space of time he had been with him – pity he had not spent more. That man could do anything with those hands of his. To rebuild the wreck would be an easy job for Antenor, a piece of honey-cake. Areon remembered the words the old man spoke that first day when he had taught him to bore through two pieces of wood to make them meet exactly so as to pin them together with pegs:

"A carpenter must have a clear mind, empty of distraction. His hand should be firm, his eye keen. He must practise patience.....Most important of all, he should have a picture, a dream...." At the time Areon had wondered what he meant by this.

Now he knew. For, as he sat there in the shadowy darkness, a vision of that little boat rose up inside him like a leaping flame; not a vision of rack and ruin; not a wreck run aground. He saw a boat, whole and new, riding the waves like a seagull free in the wind.

Chapter 18

There were a number of times that summer when the palace was quite empty of people. Games were held – foot races, horse races, javelin and discus throwing, boxing and wrestling – and everyone flocked to them. Also there were days when processions and ceremonies in honour of the gods had to be attended. Nesa and Osban looked forward to these occasions. For her it was an opportunity to relax, to go about her work without that feeling of being watched over at every turn. Likewise for Osban. However, the deserted palace also presented him with a chance to do something else, besides the pinching of the food from the kitchen.

For some time he had been hatching a scheme in his mind. A dangerous, daring scheme, he knew. He had been biding his time, waiting for the right moment. And with the arrival of the big harvest festival that moment had come.

Only the King and a few servants remained in the palace. Old Terpius had been unwell recently and so was unable to attend the celebrations. That evening, as was his custom, he rested in the shade of the courtyard garden. He would have his meal there.

Presently the servants appeared. Nesa and Osban were the first among them. She quickly drew up the small silver table to the fountain, while he spread a fine crimson cover on top. The third servant arranged the silver plates and a wine cup; the fourth placed a basket containing bread; while the last stood by with the gold mixing bowl. All of this went unnoticed by the aged King who dozed away, propped up in his silver-studded chair.

Entering the palace again the Trojans stood aside to let the three servants pass. Nesa peeped back out the door at the King. "It's well for some, to be waited on hand and foot," she sighed.

"Look who's talking," said Osban with a smart grin. "Weren't you treated like that when you were back at home? You and Areon. The pair of you had a great time up in Priam's palace. It was not like that for me. I had to work for my keep."

"Work! You never had to lift a finger," scoffed Nesa. "You used to spend the entire day playing out in the streets or running about with that over-sized dog of yours. And you never had to go to school either, like we did, did you?"

What she said was true of course, but Osban was having too much fun to admit it. "Well, if you call that 'school', I'd go there any time. From what I saw, the only lessons that Areon ever took were from that carpenter — up on the battlements all day long or down in the shed making things. And as for you, weren't you in the stables most of the time? Where's the 'school' in that?"

"You are some scoundrel," she laughed.

"Look out, I hear them coming back."

"Come, let's move."

One golden rule they had learned was to never be seen to be idling. They moved quickly down the corridor. Just as they turned the corner they met the servants again, two of them this time, bearing the King's meal of stewed squid and vegetables.

"Slippery squid! – he's welcome to it," whispered Nesa, making a face.

"I wouldn't say no to it," said Osban.

They passed the kitchen and slipped into one of the store-rooms.

"I think we could slip home early this evening," said Nesa. "Just as soon as Calchas goes."

"Why, is he still here? I thought he'd left for the ceremonies." Osban tried not to betray his concern. His plan would work only if Calchas was out of the palace.

"He'll be going soon. We can leave then. The other three won't mind anyway, all the work is done."

"I just have a bit of cleaning to do upstairs," said Osban as matter of factly as he could.

"You can leave that."

"No, I might as well get it done."

"Fine, but do it quickly… First, let's go and see – he may have left already."

They made their way quietly to the Accounts Room. The door was ajar. They peeped in. There was Calchas, sitting with his back to them, not much more than a spear's length away. Dressed in white ceremonial robes, he was still working on the tablets and scrolls set out before him on the well-polished table. Nesa held her breath. Suddenly, beside her, Osban began to shake with silent laughter.

Just as she pulled him back from the door they heard Calchas get up from the table. Instantly they separated. Nesa scurried down the corridor. Osban disappeared into the kitchen.

Osban was whistling to himself as nonchalantly as he could when Calchas passed through the kitchen. Presently he heard the loud rattle of chariot wheels on the cobblestones outside.

A moment later Nesa appeared. "You fool, you nearly gave us away," she told him.

"I couldn't help it, Nesa. Anyway, he's gone now."

"That's a relief. I'll go and hitch up the mule then."

"Good," said Osban, taking up the sponge and the bowl. "I'll hurry up with this, and I'll meet you at the gate."

"Don't be long," she reminded him again.

Osban stepped out into the corridor. He stood for a moment, stonestill. Not a sound could be heard anywhere in the palace. He went straight up to the room where Calchas had been. He gave a quick glance up and down the corridor and, as quietly as he could, opened the door. When he saw the row of keys hanging on the pegs he felt his heart quicken. His hand trembled as it reached out and took a key, the one with the ivory handle. He slipped it inside his tunic and walked out the door. *There is no turning back now,* he thought to himself.

He passed through the Great Hall where still hung the rich spicy aroma of last night's banquet. He came to the great staircase which rose in five flights to the floor where the King and his nobles had their apartments. He counted the steps as he climbed to the top. At the forty ninth and last step he stumbled, spilling the water from his bowl on to the marble floor. Breathlessly he cleaned it up with his sponge.

Only recently had he and Nesa been permitted to work in this part of the palace. They could sweep and clean and polish in the corridors but were strictly forbidden to enter any of the rooms. Shortly he was about to do something much more serious than that and his heart was in his mouth. Yet hidden within him was a seed of courage; day by day it had been growing; now as each moment passed it became stronger and stronger.

There was no point in delaying, he told himself. Trying to keep calm, he strolled along the corridor. All the doors were closed except one. As he passed by he noticed the wall brightly painted with a pair of leaping dolphins and glimpsed the corner of a large bed. A fragrance of rose petals was in the air. He moved on silently.

Coming to the end of the corridor he paused at the big open window. From the courtyard below he heard the sounds of a harp and flute – the King was taking his meal to music. Risking one peep, he saw the old man below at the table with one of the servants beside him pouring water on his hands from a silver jug. Another servant was drawing wine from a mixing bowl and pouring it into a cup. By the fountain where the water fell dancing into a green-tiled basin, two musicians stood playing. Quickly Osban drew back again.

He turned the corner and came to the door of the Treasure Room. *"Do not hesitate. Do it,"* he told himself. Immediately he put in the key and shot back the bolts. The noise of it was so loud he nearly fainted. The double doors opened before him. He stepped inside.

He looked for only one thing. He took no notice of the suit of armour that hung there, or of the polished bow made from the horns of an ibex, or the fine clothes in the presses or the silver and gold in the boxes. It was the sword that his eye fixed upon. The Sword, Echelune. Osban smiled with satisfaction. His guesswork had been correct. So here was where Megnor had hidden it away.

From generation to generation, from king to king, it had been handed down. It belonged to and was part of each and every Trojan. The unquenchable spirit of Troy, it was said, shone in its fiery gems. The unconquerable will of Troy was reflected in its gleaming blade. Its imperishable metal would forever bear witness to that glorious name. And Osban's dearest, most secret wish was to bring it home. For that he would risk everything.

He drew the Sword from its scabbard and held it before him. His hands trembled with what they held. He whispered in awe: "The Achaean shall not hold you. I, Osban, shall free you. By the blood of my people I swear it." Then he replaced the Sword and left.

Nesa was waiting for him outside the Gate as arranged.

"What's up with you?" she asked. "You're very serious looking. What have you been doing up there?" Nesa was like that, she could so easily unfold a person.

"Nothing," he replied, climbing on to the cart. "Quick, let's get out of here before we meet the procession."

"Nothing?" she smiled, taking up the reins. "Come now, there must be something… a few more cakes perhaps?"

"No, nothing this time, I'm afraid," he said coolly.

"You're getting very serious, Osban," she jested. "And secretive too, like Areon. You'd never know what he's up to either."

"Well, maybe he'll tell us. I had a feeling last time there was something he wanted to talk about," said Osban.

"I wonder has he got something up his sleeve?" said Nesa.

They were not able to avoid the procession however. Driving the mule into the town, they found the road ahead blocked as it passed, winding its way towards the temple.

"Take up the axe in your hands," Nesa told him at once. She had brought the axe with her for this very purpose, so they could pretend they were going for firewood if questioned.

"Good thinking," said Osban.

They stopped behind some spectators and waited. They saw the knights ride by, their helmets reflecting the last of the sun's

golden rays. Marching behind came two long columns of foot soldiers, their every shield brightly blazoned with eagles, hawks, panthers,lions and snakes. Then came the athletes in fresh white tunics – it was they who led the beasts of sacrifice, a pair of snow-white oxen. Next, the musicians with lyres, flutes and cymbals, and then the singers who so loudly chanted their hymn. Following behind came a great mass of people, young and old, some bearing flowers, some holding green branches aloft, and some with baskets of food. Osban gave a little wave to Pero and Nestor when he spotted them among the crowd.

"I think we ought to take another trip to the harbour later on," whispered Nesa as she watched the procession move away.

"Why?" asked Osban. They had spied on the harbour only two nights previously.

"Because there will be feasting and drinking again tonight – this will be the third night of it – and I'd be surprised if the guard does not slip at the harbour. It would serve us to find out."

"But remember we have to meet up with Areon again in a few nights," said Osban, who loved his sleep and was not exactly alight at the prospect of yet another midnight excursion to the harbour.

"I know, we're going to be tired. I think it might be worth it though."

"Maybe."

"Will you come then?"

"Yes, of course."

Chapter 19

Megnor had had enough of the harvest festivities, his head was sore from them. He picked up the lionskin, threw it around his shoulders and took up his javelin. The skin was his latest trophy and he wore it with pride. Today he would ride alone to that valley again. If one lion had crossed from the mainland perhaps there was another, he thought. If there was, he might try to take it by himself. The prospect of it excited him, reminding him of that feeling of danger he knew so well in war. He missed the war sometimes, he had to admit to himself.

He went first to the Treasure Room. It pleased him just to stand there, to look over the spoils he had brought home. *"And there is more elsewhere,"* he smiled gloatingly. Two more boxes he had hidden in secret places known only to himself and Calchas. The precautions had to be taken, there were so few whom he felt could trust. Danger could strike from within or without at any time, he believed; loyal subjects could turn behind one's back; treachery or greed could so easily poison the hearts of former allies.

But it was late in the morning and there was no time to linger. He took the curved bow from the wall, slung it on his shoulders and hurried from the room.

As he crossed the courtyard he passed Nesa who was coming from the stables. Unknown to him she had just been to feed his horse a handful of nuts. She had made this her habit each morning, for she felt for the beast, this majestic creature that had once roamed so free on the plain of Troy. It, like her, had been cruelly seized and carried away. Unlike her, however, it had no chance of ever returning, and the thought of that wounded her.

Megnor glanced at her as she walked away with quickening steps. Much less could he trust a Trojan, he felt. She and her friend, the plump one, always seemed to be slinking about the place, scarcely doing any work as far as he could make out. It was time to put a stop to it and tell Calchas to find some real work for them. And what about the other one, the fellow who tended the sheep? – Zeus knows what he could be up to! After the hunting today he might pay him a visit. "Never trust a Trojan. Horse-taming is all they were ever good for," he said to himself as he entered the stables.

That same morning, as Megnor rode out, Areon stood back and looked at his boat. He felt pleased with himself, proud of what he had done in such a short space of time. He had been working steadily for many days. Now only two more planks remained to get completed and the boat would be whole again, reborn with a glowing body of pale yellow wood.

It had not been easy though, he recalled. Before even beginning repairs there had been the problem of having to haul the vessel back behind the shelter of a large outcrop of rock where he could work in peace and security. How long it had taken to dig a channel through the sand! How long to make smooth rollers to lay in it! Then six big rams needed to be fastened together and tied with ropes to the vessel. To get the thing to shift at all had been a terrible struggle. But once on top of the rollers it had moved with much less difficulty. The task had taken him the best part of four days.

With the vessel in place he had begun work in earnest. He

felled a number of trees which were dead at the roots and whose timber would be light and dry. He trimmed them, smoothed them and began cutting them into planks. Meanwhile, he searched for oak bushes and from its branches made nails to pin the timber together. The nailing of the planks was, he found, the hardest part of all. Many slots had first to be cut into the edge of the planks, with great care being taken to ensure that each and every slot on a plank corresponded exactly with that on the next. He then inserted little tongues of wood into the slots to join the planks together. Finally, he bored holes and drove in the nails to hold the tongues in place.

Plank by plank he had built it up from the keel. Little by little the vessel had taken shape. The task had been enormous, but he had been patient and painstaking, and it had borne fruit.

"Only two more planks and she will be done," he said to himself as he stood there admiring his craftsmanship. "Two more planks **and a coating of pitch**," he had to remind himself.

Right from the beginning he had felt that the pitch-making could be a problem. He had seen it made once at home in Troy and it looked anything but simple. The easy part was to collect the sticky resin from the pine trees. He had already gashed some trees for this purpose. No, the hard part was to make the right kind of fire to heat the resin. He remembered how in Troy they had piled the wood so high and so wide and then covered it all with sods of earth. *"Why did they have to do it like that?"* he wondered now.

He remembered also how a channel had been made at the base of the pile to collect the pitch. The first liquid given off by the fire was, he was told, used to flavour wines; the next was used for medicines. The final liquid to trickle out was the pitch.

"Not an easy job, not an easy job at all. But we'll manage one way or another, won't we Teg?" he said, stroking the little dog. "Now, where has Kaela gone?"

He picked up his tools and headed back across the slopes to the sheep.

His thoughts turned to his friends whom he would be meeting the following night. *"It is time to tell them. I have kept it from them long enough. Things will have to move quickly now."*

He had released the flock at dawn and found them scattered along the bubbling course of the stream that ran down to the cave. Only a few were still feeding away on the sparse grass, the others were resting in the shade of the rocks. *"I'll get something to eat first. Then I'll repair the rest of that wall. After that I'll bring them up to the little glen and relax for the rest of the afternoon,"* he decided.

However, as happened quite often these days, a spot of fishing intervened between these plans and the wall outside the cave remained untouched. It was late afternoon before he set off for that favourite place of his in the hills...

*　*　*　*　*　*　*　*　*　*　*

There was no other lion in the valley or anywhere else, Megnor felt certain of that. Not even a deer had crossed his path; his two hounds had wandered off; it had been a frustrating day.

Having come this far he thought he might as well seek out and inspect his flock. He was uneasy about that Trojan boy, all alone here without supervision. The other pair in the palace were too close for comfort; this fellow was too far away. Calchas would have to be told. Now that he thought of it he was glad he had not returned with any more slaves. The very thought of being surrounded by Trojans made him feel uncomfortable.

He would have to hurry though. Time was against him. There were more important things still to attend to back at the palace. He spurred the horse and drove him hard up the track to the top of the ridge.

Areon, meanwhile, had come to the glen with his animals. He was sitting on his rock beside the pool, with Teg stretched out nearby – the little dog was worn out after the usual morning's games with Kaela. The cub was not to be seen. A short while earlier she had been splashing about happily in the pool as she always did whenever they came here. Then, after rolling about in the long dry grass, she had gone to one of her 'scratching trees'. These were the two or three trees which she regularly used to scratch with her claws, leaving deep lines in the bark. Why she did this, he did not know. Perhaps to sharpen them, he thought.

He was on the point of calling out for the lion when he saw the horseman. In an instant he knew who it was. It shocked him to find Megnor so close, suddenly appearing out of nowhere like a ghost. As the Achaean rode down towards him he stood up glancing from side to side, searching for any sign of Kaela. He was fearful for the cub.

"Greetings, your lordship," said Areon and bowed. "*I must try and get rid of him as quickly as possible,*" came the thought.

Megnor did not acknowledge him, only sat there on the horse looking around at the sheep. Yet when at last he spoke it was not unfriendly:

"You are taking good care of all my sheep then. Are you, boy?"

"Yes, my lord," said Areon, relieved that at least Megnor could see the animals were in good condition.

"And you keep them well at night?"

"I have them penned in the cave where I sleep, lordship." Just then he spotted something moving in the branches of a tree directly behind Megnor. Kaela! The cub must have been resting up there and now – to Areon's horror – was trying to climb down.

"Have you had any trouble with them?"

"Trouble? lordship." He could not believe what his eyes saw. That daft lion! He tried not to look, tried to pretend it was not happening.

"Has any wild beast ever bothered them?"

"No, your lordship. Never," said Areon. The cub was having difficulty getting down, he could see. *Stay where you are, you silly beast!* his thoughts silently urged.

"If you see anything you are to send word to me immediately, is that understood, boy?"

"Yes, my lord," Areon nodded. Kaela was balanced precariously between two branches, teetering on the edge of disaster. *"She's going to fall, she's going to fall!"* raced thoughts to the beat of his heart.

"And in the meantime take good care of my sheep."

"Yes, my lord," he answered, barely able to pass the word from his lips.

Then to his immense relief Megnor turned and rode away.

Areon watched him as he went. Only now did he think of the boat, of the danger that Megnor might discover it, and he wondered which way he would ride next. There was no need to worry however, for the Achaean rode up to the brow of the hill and headed away northwards and homewards.

Turning to Kaela, he was just in time to see her tumbling from the tree. Wounded in pride if not in body the lion came over to him and rubbed her head against his leg in greeting. Not to be out-done, Teg sprang to his feet, tail-a-wagging, and came to lick his hands. Areon put his arms around the two and held them close.

Chapter 20

Nesa went alone to the meeting at the hut the following night. Osban had complained of feeling unwell earlier in the day and she had made him stay behind. Walking across the moonlit hill she worried over once more having to bring Areon the disappointing news from the latest trip to the harbour. The prospects of an escape seemed as remote as ever.

When he told her of his boat she could scarcely believe it:

"Are you serious? Where? How far from here?" she wanted to know.

"It's some distance down the coast."

"I want to see it. Bring me to it."

"It's too far away for that," he replied. He did not want her to see the boat just yet.

"Well, I'll have to see it. What sort of state is it in?"

"Very good, really quite good. Not much needed to be done with it," he lied, without even thinking.

"And what did you have to do?" she inquired, eyeing him keenly.

He suspected that if he told her the full truth about the state of the wreck when he found it she might be very wary of the whole idea. He replied:

"Just one or two side planks had to be replaced and a few things like that."

"And are you sure this boat will float on the water, let alone sail?"

"Of course, I'm sure." But deep down, if he would admit it, he was not sure. Certainly, sometimes he looked at the boat and it seemed well-built, whole, pleasing to the eye. There were other times, however, when he examined his work and perceived only flaws and weaknesses. He did not like that feeling. It was some thing he wanted to fight against. He told her: "This boat, I'll guarantee, is as sound, if not sounder than any of the boats in that harbour down there."

"I hope you're right," Nesa said. And she went on to ask him a thousand questions about the vessel – how did he come by it? what did it look like? how long was it? how wide? and so on and so forth. He was exhausted by the end of it.

Finally, she just looked at him, grinned broadly and said: "It seems to me you know what you are doing, Areon. If you are happy with it, then so are we. When are we sailing home then?"

"Sooner than you think. I'm almost finished."

"When, Areon?" she persisted.

"All I need to do is make some pitch."

"That's not going to be easy."

"It might take a while to get it right," he shrugged.

"There is an easier solution," said Nesa, clicking her fingers. "One or two of the smaller boats in the harbour are not coated with pitch at all, at least not with the black stuff. They're painted white – have you not noticed?"

"No; I don't understand."

"The stuff they take from the trees – the sticky stuff, what's it called?"

"Resin."

"Yes, the resin, correct. I've seen them mix it with lime, that's all. Then they coat their boats with it. Simple, eh? And quick."

"You're a genius, Nesa. Can you get me some of this lime?" Areon asked.

"Andraemon has some. I could bring it tomorrow."

"Great."

"If I did, how soon would you have the boat ready?"

"The moon will be full in a couple of days, I'd have her right by then."

"That's settled. If you have it ready, we'll be ready."

It was with a lighter step and a brighter heart that she returned to the homestead that night.

She knew she had to talk to Andraemon. *"Strike while the iron is hot,"* she said to herself. And the following evening she went to him.

He was sitting, as he always sat at night, crosslegged beside the fire, bent over the piece of wood he was carving.

"How is our friend, Osban, feeling this night?" he asked of her as she sat down opposite.

"Much better. He said to tell you that the rabbit was delicious – he ate every scrap of it."

Andraemon chuckled. "He must be improving so."

"He'll be able to go back to work tomorrow, I think."

"Well, only if he feels up to it. If not, I can go and speak with Calchas again. He is not an unreasonable man at times, he will understand."

"Thank you, Andraemon." *Don't beat about the bush,* she told herself. *Ask him straight out, ask him now.* She cleared her throat, twice. "Andraemon..." she began.

"Yes?" He looked up at her, still whittling away with his knife.

"There is something I want to talk to you about..."

"Yes?" he nodded.

"We were wondering.... myself and Areon and Osban, that is.....we wanted to ask you... you see, we have decided to..." She cleared her throat again. "We have decided..."

"To run away," he finished it for her.

"How did you know!" she gasped.

"Andraemon is no fool, he notices things," he told her with a wink of his eye.

"Will you come, Andraemon? We have a boat. Come with us."

He put down the knife and the wood. His expression changed, becoming serious. He looked at her with a close, penetrating eye, then looked away into the flames of the pinewood fire. When he spoke at last his voice sounded very distant. "It was kind of you to think of me. I'm glad that you have told me."

"But will you come, Andraemon?"

"No."

"Why not?" she asked in disbelief.

He did not answer.

"Why not, Andraemon? Why won't you come?" she asked again. "Everything is prepared. We've got a plan. We know what we're doing. We are going to get away from here, believe me."

"I'm sure you will. I pray that you will," he said softly. "But Andraemon cannot come with you."

"Don't you want to get away from here? Don't you want to see your family again?" She was exasperated, she could not accept that he would not want to come.

"I am old....too long away....too long a slave. My name is forgotten. There can be no going back. It is not possible to step into the same river twice."

"That is not so."

"I know it is hard for you to understand."

"I do not understand, Andraemon," said Nesa sharply. She had never spoken to him in this way before, but she was almost angry with him now. "That very first day we met, you told us how wretched was the life of a slave. I can't believe that you want to live this life of misery. There is a choice now. Yes, it's a chance too, but a chance worth taking. Surely you do not want to stay here? I just don't understand it."

"You will understand, believe me."

"Listen to me, Andraemon –"

"No, Nesa," he interrupted her, "I'm telling you; I will not come. I thank you for thinking of me. I cannot come with you." He took up the knife and wood in his hands again, though he did not continue carving; his eyes returned to the flames and were far away once more.

Nesa got to her feet. "It is your decision," she sighed. "However, I feel that you should think about it some more."

Not wanting to go to bed just yet, she walked up the path through the pines. The night air was cold, she pulled the cloak around herself and stepped quickly over rocks that were silvery in the moonlight. She wanted, needed to see that moon again and to view the starry heavens. Yet the picture of Andraemon, sitting alone beside the fire, kept coming into her mind.

She came out of the line of trees and looked up. There in the east she saw Orion the Hunter and scattered around him the animals he forever chased – the Hare, the Bull, the Unicorn and the Lion. She saw the Great Bear, and counted again the Pleiades, the ones her father called the Seven Sisters. She remembered those occasions when he used to bring her and her little sisters and brother up to the roof of their apartment to view the sky at night. How expertly he read the stars and how well he told their story. Then she smiled to herself and thought; *"But somehow, I think, he must have got it wrong about these Seven Sisters, for I'm sure there are at least eight of them!"*

When at last the moon peeped out from behind the solitary silver cloud above the hill, she felt her spirits rise. *"Maybe, just maybe,"* she thought, *"they are out on the roof tonight looking at this moon and these stars and thinking of me – thinking of me, as I stand here looking up and thinking of them."* And in this moment she gave not a thought to her fears for her family or to the terrible tales of Troy's destruction, for in her heart she trusted that all would be well.

Yet still the picture of Andraemon sitting alone beside the fire kept coming into her mind. *"What is stopping him from joining us?"* she asked herself again. As she gazed serenely at the broad pale face of the moon above she thought of how year after year he had lived the life of a slave, a life without hope. And in some way she began to understand.

Chapter 21

At last the day had dawned. Yawning, Areon rose, placed a few pieces of dry wood on the ashes of the fire and huddled down over it, blowing softly, breathing new life into embers which reddened and sparked to a mysterious flame. In the darkness he heard the lion get up to come to him and felt the greeting of her rough tongue on his leg. Lying next to him were two sticks of ash-wood which he had cut and trimmed some days previously. He now sharpened both to a point with his knife. Immediately he put the sticks into the flames to harden them.

Had he not been taken away, he would this autumn have taken part in the Ceremony of Arms, the first step to becoming a warrior. With others of his age he would have stood before King Priam in the Assembly Place to be touched on the forehead with the Sword and to be presented with his shield and javelin. Before the King, before his family and before all the people of Troy, he would have taken the oath to defend his city.

He withdrew the two blackened points from the fire and held the weapons before him. Then he spoke those words he remembered so well:

"I pledge this to my people: Around my waist I shall buckle the belt of Loyalty. Steadfastness shall be the breastplate I wear.

I pledge this to my King: Honour shall be my helmet, and Truth the shield I hold.

I pledge this to the Deathless Ones: Mercy shall be the sword I carry."

Leaving the cave and climbing the slope, he listened to the wild screeching of the gulls and the wild tumbling beat of the stream swollen with yesterday's rain. Higher and higher he went until he reached the top of the ridge. Then he stopped to look. The moon was still to be seen, hung like a pale lantern in the room of the world. Turning, he looked to the south, following the dark line of the mainland to where it ended and where the void of the sea and sky began. Here was the gateway to freedom. The thought of it terrified him, thrilled him.

He thought of all the times he had gazed like this in the past, all the times he had stood looking out over the waves, caught between hope and despair. But there would be no more standing, no more gazing, he told himself. Tonight it would happen. Tonight he would strike for freedom. The idea of it made him want to shout, no, to roar.

A real urge to run gripped him. Down he went, like a wheeling, diving seagull. Down with the tumbling stream he flew, and the roar he gave rose above the roar of any stream or the cry of any gull. With furious speed he descended on to the beach and threw himself on the sand. He lay on his back, panting. He lay there for a long time, until his body was as still and his mind and heart as clear as the sky above him.

*   *   *   *   *   *   *   *   *   *   *

Osban also was looking into the sky that morning as he rode from the homestead to the palace for what he prayed would be the last time. But he may as well have been looking at his feet, for his mind was buzzing with thoughts, his heart was beating fast, and he hardly heard a word of what Nesa said as she drove the mule beside him.

Yesterday he had put the Sword away. It had been a masterly operation, he thought with satisfaction. He pictured it again now in his mind – the empty palace, the open door, the key hanging there in Calchas's office…

"I'm glad Andraemon was up to bid us farewell this morning," Nesa was saying. "I would not have liked to have left without seeing him. And that food he gave us will be very useful."

…Like a mouse he had slipped into the Treasure Room. Like a shadow he had passed down the corridor and stairs with the Sword in the rug. Gliding out by the side door he had crossed the small courtyard to the stables. Quickly he had put it away, burying it under the straw in the corner…

"I feel sorry for that man, he has been so good to us," continued Nesa. "He was asking me about the boat again yesterday evening. He seemed so interested in it I thought he might change his mind. But no, he will not change. There is no sense to it."

Osban was not listening to her. *"It was all so easy,"* he was thinking to himself. *"All I had to do was beat the dust from the rug for a few moments, go back inside, replace the key and leave the rug back upstairs. Masterly!"*

"He still has time to change his mind if he wants to. Do you think he might?" she asked.

"I have saved the Sword. No thief like Megnor will ever lay hands on it again. I wonder what my people will say when they see me return with it."

"Osban! you are not listening to me. Are you still asleep or what?"

"I'm sorry. I was thinking of something."

"Well listen to me: wake up and keep alert. You are going to have to keep your wits about you today – today above all days," she told him.

"I know that, Nesa." *If only she knew. I can't wait to show her the Sword when we ride out of here this evening. And Areon too,* he thought.

And onwards they rode towards the towering wall of the palace.

*　　*　　*　　*　　*　　*　　*　　*　　*　　*　　*

Areon led the sheep to the pasture and left them there. Now that he was no longer their shepherd he wondered what they would do when he did not return for them this evening. Would they drift and scatter among the hills? No, most likely they would stay where they were, where there was a plentiful supply of grass and water, he figured. Either way it did not trouble him because he knew that they would come to no harm. For so many days and nights he had watched over these animals and had come to know them well. He could recognise any one of them at a glance. He had even given names to each. But he would not miss them, he had to admit.

Someone else would have to be the shepherd, someone else the slave. From now on he would carry a spear not a staff. He was unchained and free – wild, free and Trojan.

He then went to bring some food and water to store in the boat, and the few blankets Andraemon had given him. Yesterday he had hauled it out from its hiding place and down to the edge of the sea. Looking at it now, covered with pitch and finished at last, he felt he had done his best with it and was confident that Nesa and Osban would be impressed. But how would it fare out on the high seas? – That was the question. Time would tell and there was no point in worrying about it, he told himself again.

There was little else to do but wait. He returned to the cave and fixed himself something to eat.

Later he played on the beach with Teg and Kaela, throwing sticks for them. Teg as usual dutifully fetched and returned each stick whereas that crazy lion ran away with them. Afterwards he sat on the sand and the little dog came and sat next to him, as he always did. Teg had been such a good friend all those long lonely days and nights, and it pained him to have to leave him behind. "Good boy, good fellow," he said and he patted him and stroked his long ears.

Then he picked up a sharp stone and went into the cave, for he intended to put the mark of his name on its wall. However, no sooner had he begun this than he decided against it. He threw away the stone disdainfully. "I will leave nothing behind me, not even my name," he declared.

There was nothing else to do but wait, and waiting he found hard. Low banks of cloud came in from the west blotting out the progress of the sun. Rings of foam drifted on the tide, and in the rock pools numberless ripples raced and mingled in dreamlike patterns. Seagulls glided silently on the uprising air. Slowly, slowly the day seemed to pass.

At last he could stand it no longer. He took up his spear, called the dog and the lion and set out for the meeting place.

*   *   *   *   *   *   *   *   *   *   *

It was late afternoon and still there was a line of people in the courtyard. Nesa had been watching them come throughout the day: the fishermen, the labourers, weavers, bakers, potters, cobblers, coppersmiths, all the ordinary people of the island.

Yesterday they had delivered their quotas to the royal stores; today in return they queued to receive their share of oil, grain or wine from the King. Dressed in colourless clothes they stood patiently before the big table while the unhurried palace clerk and the storemaster carefully recorded every detail and slowly gave every measure. Nesa wished that she could be as patient.

When the courtyard was cleared and the shadows begun to fall, then she would make the move.

She had hardly seen Osban all day. He had gone about his own duties; she had carried out hers – that way they would not draw attention to themselves. All that was left for her to do was to go to the spring for water.

She was lifting the tall jars on to the cart when he appeared.

"Not much time left now, Nesa," he said, giving her that mischievous grin again.

"Be quiet, will you," she told him tensely.

"We'll be laughing out on the high seas tonight, eh? You, me and Areon – the Trojan pirates!" he whispered in her ear, rubbing his hands gleefully.

"There's not a nervous bone in your body, is there?"

"No. But I'm wondering when we can leave here, it's getting late, and my feet are beginning to itch."

"You know the plan as well as I do. Wait till I come back with the water and we'll see."

"All right."

"Now move along and look busy," she told him.

"See you in a while," he nodded and off he went whistling.

She sat up on the mulecart and rode across the courtyard. Calchas was there now hovering around his clerks at the tables. High on the battlements the guards seemed relaxed, chatting to one another. Shortly everybody would be leaving for the festival celebrations.

As she neared the gate she heard someone calling her name. She turned and saw Pero smiling at her from the line of people. Nesa waved back and rode out the gate.

Osban went straight to the stables. The time to move the Sword was fast approaching. In truth he was nervous, not at all as he pretended to Nesa.

Walking into the stable his whistling stopped abruptly when he saw Megnor, with his back turned, standing by his horse. In a panic he turned and fled.

    *   *   *   *   *   *   *   *   *   *   *

The meeting place was to be at the end of the valley where Areon had first minded the sheep. On his way there he had stopped at the chestnut woods to gather a bundle of sticks for the small beacon-fire he intended to light for his friends. Half-way up on the rocky slope he settled himself down to wait under the shelter of a large boulder and began carefully arranging the pile of wood before him. Teg lay next to him, while Kaela was perched on the rocky ledge above, as if on look-out. Nesa and Osban would not be too long in coming, he hoped.

The blanket of cloud on the sky was the cause of some concern to him, as was the mist that was beginning to drift in over the hills. Moonlight would be minimal, navigation would be difficult, he feared.

Then he felt the first fleck of rain on his cheek. He looked up and complained aloud at his ill-luck.

    *   *   *   *   *   *   *   *   *   *   *

The crowd in the courtyard had dwindled to five or six, and Calchas had left for the temple. The sentries were in the tower sheltering from the rain, and in the courtyard below only Megnor's squire was standing to attention, by his master's horse. The young man stood somewhat nervously awaiting the return of Megnor who had just stormed back into the palace for the ceremonial dagger he had forgotten, cursing the delay and swearing at the rain.

The moment Megnor entered the Treasure Room he knew the sword was missing and he knew who had taken it. "I should never have trusted a Trojan," he spat out venomously. Calmly, coldly, he lifted the whip from the peg.

Osban had seen Pero in the courtyard and had gone to talk with her. He found it hard to give her his full attention, though, and his eyes kept straying to the gate in expectation of Nesa's return. Thus he was not to notice the look of fear that slowly spread across her face as she watched Megnor strolling towards them gently tapping the whip in his hand.

Megnor glided in closer. Pero stepped back. Before Osban knew it he had been knocked to the ground. He heard the whip whistle as it cut through the air and felt it burn across his legs like a red-hot knife. Before it had come down again he was squealing like a terrified animal. In horror Pero ran to the open gate.

Megnor struck him then the second and the third time. Curled up on the ground, protecting his head, Osban only heard that voice that lashed him like the whip.

"Listen well to what I say, boy, and make it easy on yourself... or else you'll have to listen to this!" down came the whip again, slashing the earth close to his face. "Either you tell me where you've hidden that sword or I'll beat you until you do. And I'll

beat that friend of yours as well, is that clear? Is that clear?...
WHERE HAVE YOU PUT THE SWORD, BOY?" the voice suddenly exploded.

Even Nesa, who was at that moment riding up to the gate,
heard it.

Pero came running down to her waving her arms fearfully.
"Go back! Go back, don't go in there. He's mad, he'll whip you
too," she warned.

"Is it Osban?....."

"Yes. I can't stay....must go," said the terrified girl, and she
ran away through the misty veil of rain.

But Pero had only gone forty paces when something made
her stop. She turned and looked back.

Nesa's knees were shaking as she got down from the mulecart. Stepping up to the side of the gate, she peeped in. Before her
she saw the limp bundle that was Osban lying face down in the
dirt. She was so close to him she could hear him whimpering.
The Achaean was standing over him, fists clenched, menacing.

"That sword better be where you've said it is," she heard him
threaten. "You, come here," he called to his squire. The young
man let go of the horse and sprang to his master's command,
"Keep a close watch on him till I come back." And with that
Megnor marched off to the stables.

Nesa felt so weak she could hardly stand. Sinking to her
knees, she buried her head in her hands. *What can I do? What can
I do?"* she screamed inside.

Again she heard that awful whimpering cry from Osban. She
pressed her hands against her ears, but she could not block out
the pain that sound produced in her.

At that very moment she heard the words of inspiration:

"Nesa, the horse!" – her friend, Pero, who had come back now stood beside her.

"Nesa, the horse – go on, take it!" Pero's words cut through the darkness like a beam of pure sunlight.

At once Nesa stood up and stood out in the gateway. It amazed her to find the horse already coming towards her as if answering a call. She looked over to Pero. Her friend smiled, nodded encouragement.

She stepped towards the animal.

Sensing something, Osban awoke from his nightmare of fear. A glance at the figure mounting the horse near the gate was sufficient. In one lightning movement he seized the moment and the legs of his guard. The young squire came crashing to the ground and Osban was up and running. No one who knew him would have recognised this same boy who now moved with the swiftness of the wind and leapt, as if no earthly force withheld him, on to the stallion's back.

"Away with you!" cried out Nesa as she snapped forward the reins.

Out of the prison-fortress they swept, leaving behind the startled cries of the guards. Like a caged bird which suddenly finds its way unbarred and, crazy for freedom, wildly takes wing into the limitless sky, so the horse flew out into the wide and the open.

Osban clung fiercely to Nesa. But she scarcely gripped the reins, instead she gave the horse its head – she could not do otherwise, for the animal galloped with an unstoppable power.

Down into the town they fled. Madly they galloped through its streets sending startled citizens scurrying for safety. Then out by the long road they thundered, that same road they had travelled so often so slowly, now disappearing beneath them in the twinkling of an eye. Nearing the crossroads Nesa finally reined in the beast. With a flick of her wrist she turned him into the fields.

They came to the river. The horse splashed its entry and bore them across the swirling flood. The sudden heave as they climbed out on to the bank sent Osban tumbling from the animal, almost bringing Nesa with him. Back into the muddy waters he fell. The cold shock of it stunned him momentarily and he lay there wide-eyed and open-mouthed, chest-deep in the flood.

"Can't you ever hold on to anything!" Nesa screamed at him.

"Shut up! Shut up!" he roared back, and struck himself with his fists in fury. He scrambled out like a madman and struggled up the steep bank after her. Just as he was trying to mount the horse again he spotted the pursuer. The rider had left the road and was coming straight towards them. Osban's spirit quailed. He felt the strength drain from every muscle and fibre of his body.

"He's coming," he was barely able to say.

"Get up! Get up!" bellowed Nesa.

He tried to haul himself up on the horse but his arms were like water, his feet like clay. Fear had rooted him to the ground.

"Get up on the horse, Osban," said Nesa now in a strangely calm yet ferocious voice. Her hand reached out and clasped his collar and pulled him up. Once more they were away.

A few moments later the dark figure of Megnor loomed up large in the mist on the other side of the river.

Moving like the wind, the Trojans cut through the grove of yellow poplars and made for the hill. *"If we could only get to the valley we might lose him,"* thought Nesa. But the slope was becoming steeper and steeper and the horse was tiring. Desperately she urged him on.

Osban clung to Nesa, not daring to open his eyes – he did not need eyes to tell him that the pursuer was pressing hard, drawing them back little by little. Still, somehow, they made it to the top of the ridge. Headlong into the valley they went.

In a breath Megnor appeared. He drew to a halt. His horse reared up, neighing wildly. He knew he had the measure of them now and he smiled grimly. He drew the Sword. With a savage cry he spurred his animal into final pursuit.

The Trojan horse was struggling, slowing. Relentlessly the hunter closed in on his prey. Nesa saw that there was nowhere to go, nothing to do but face the oppressor.

As she reined in the horse Osban opened his eyes just in time to glimpse the figure moving out from behind the bush on his left. Areon moved with the stealth of a panther. Then he made to pounce at the enemy.

But the move was too soon, a fraction too soon, and Megnor had spotted it. Now the Sword glistened as it was raised high in the air.

But for Kaela it would have been the end.

She sprang from the undergrowth and charged the attacker. The terrified horse turned away violently and Megnor was thrown to the ground. There he lay, senseless and still.

Areon snatched up the Sword. "Hurry, give me the reins! We must tie him up," he called out to his friends.

Quickly the long straps were removed from the horse and Megnor was bound tightly, hand and foot.

They stood back then, staring in disbelief at their captive and in amazement at the lion who stood so proudly with her paws placed firmly on his chest.

"You're some lion!" said Areon breathlessly.

"Why don't you eat him, Kaela? or take a bite out of him at least?" invited Osban, beaming.

"I think she'd prefer a fish," said Nesa and they laughed.

Crumpled up on the ground, Megnor had a strangely peaceful expression on his face – like a child asleep, Nesa thought.

"He's going to get some surprise when he wakes up," she added.

"I hope I never get to see his face again," said Osban.

"Don't worry, you won't," Areon told him. "Now let's get out of here."

And so they left him there.

"You're all wet. What happened to you?" Areon asked his friend as they made their way up the slope.

"I took a tumble at the river, I'm afraid."

"That's not all you took today, was it?" muttered Nesa.

"What?" countered Osban, pretending not to hear.

"Oh nothing," she replied sweetly.

"Not to worry, Osban, I have some dry clothes put away in the boat," said Areon.

"Let's move then," said Osban, hurrying them along.

Yet they had not reached the top of the slope before Megnor came to himself. For a moment he simply lay, staring at the sky with cold, beady eyes. Suddenly, swearing between clenched teeth, he began to roll, kick and jerk about in the dirt as he struggled to break the bonds that held him.

Chapter 22

Daylight had almost faded by the time they came over the headland to the little beach. The instant Osban spotted the boat he forgot about his tiredness or his wet clothes and raced down, whooping for joy, with the dog and the lion hot on his heels.

"Come back, Teg," called Areon, and at once the dutiful dog obeyed.

"Will you not take him with us?" asked Nesa.

"I'd love to, but he's not mine," he replied. "I hate having to leave him behind."

"I know," nodded Nesa, thinking of the horse she had left in the valley.

"Nesa, come quickly, look at the boat, it's perfect!" Osban called out.

She left Areon alone with his dog and skipped off down to the shore. Osban was already on board with Kaela, both of them leaping about, one as excited as the other.

"Look at it, it's as good as new," he enthused.

Nesa walked through the knee-deep water to the side of the boat. She ran her eyes cautiously along the planking and pressed her fingers against the pitch between the lower planks. Then she climbed aboard. "I hope he has sealed it well," she said, though she was impressed by what she saw.

"What's keeping Areon?" asked Osban, unable to contain his excitement. "Let's go. Let's get out of here. Let's move!"

"Hold your horses," laughed Nesa. "Don't you think we ought to hoist up the sail first!"

"Hurry up, Areon," pleaded Osban loudly.

Areon did not need to be told that it was time to move. He stooped down to pet the faithful dog one last time. To his astonishment the dog suddenly yelped and sprang out of his way. Someone was coming. Areon wheeled around. Scarcely ten paces away stood a figure wrapped in semi-darkness. Instinctively he reached for the Sword at his side. But the deep sound of a chuckle completely disarmed him:

"Hold onto that sword, lad, you might need it."

"Andraemon, it's you," he gasped.

"It is he," came the reply. "And in the nick of time too, by the looks of it."

"I can't tell you how glad I am to –."

"You'll have to save that for later, lad," the swineherd interrupted. "There are riders in the valley beyond – heading this way. I think we had better hurry." And with that he swept up the excited dog with one hand, and the big cloth bundle at his foot with the other, and strode towards the boat.

"Not Megnor again – I don't believe it!" groaned Areon. He sprinted past Andraemon and clambered on board.

"They are still a little way off. We might be able to give them the slip," said Andraemon as he stepped into the water.

It was all too much for poor Osban whose excitement instantly became shot through with panic. He rushed to the bow, unable to contain himself. "Hoist the sail! Hoist the sail!" he screamed.

"Sit down and be quiet," said Areon, yet he could feel his own heart beating like a hammer once more.

"Do not hoist any sail yet – not till we round that headland – the wind is against us," ordered Andraemon. Then he heaved with all his might, inching the vessel forward.

"Come on, move, please move!" Osban cried out, frantically beating his fist into the palm of his hand.

"You fell off the tree; you fell off the horse; and you'll fall off this boat as well, if you're not careful," Nesa warned him.

She sat down opposite Areon on the rowing bench and quickly fixed her oar in the leather strap. Areon fumbled with his.

"Take it easy. There's no need to panic yet," she tried to assure him.

"No need to panic? – you can't be serious," he replied. "If they see us, we're finished. They'll have a ship after us in no time." He tugged again at the ill-fitting strap.

"Here, let me do it," she offered.

"Hurry, Areon, let's go," begged Osban. Even the lion and the dog were looking at him now with concern.

"If you say that one more time, it'll be me who'll toss you overboard," said Areon, sounding like he meant it.

"Yes, settle down and be quiet, young Osban," said Andraemon, waist deep in the waves and still pushing. He looked back to the ridge for any sign of the Achaeans. "If we clear the headland we'll be safely out of view. Pull hard now, we can make it." Then he jumped up on board and grabbed hold of the steering oar.

At once Areon and Nesa dipped their oars in the sea and pulled together with all their strength. At last the little boat began to glide away from the shore.

Andraemon nodded with approval as he watched them throw up the water with each stroke. "The boat is sound, she moves well. You are to be congratulated, Areon," he said,

Areon was too distracted to respond.

Not another word was spoken now. Osban, head down, sat between the lion and the dog, an arm around each; Nesa had her eyes fixed on the ridge; Andraemon, too, peering back over his shoulder as he steered the little vessel through the blackening sea. Areon, however, kept his eyes closed, bit his lips and counted every stroke.

When he finally dared to look back, it surprised him how far they had come. The dark mass of the mountain ridge was gone, only the jagged cliffs of the headland loomed threateningly.

"We're safe, he'll not see us now," he said, breaking the silence.

"So far so good," Nesa replied with satisfaction.

"Forget about Megnor, keep pulling hard," Andraemon interrupted them. "We're not home and dry yet, or anywhere near it." His voice betrayed real concern, for the wind was rising stronger by the moment, the sea becoming more and more agitated.

Darkness descended swiftly, the rain began to pelt.

As they rounded the headland the great ocean opened up before them with an unexpected suddenness, heaving and churning violently. The little boat which up to this had moved with the sureness of a footsoldier, now began to reel like a drunkard, tottering backwards one moment, tilting violently forwards the next, as wave upon wave snatched it up, hurled it on high and dropped it down.

With a sudden almighty thunder-crash a lightning bolt streaked from the heavens, lighting up the world. In that awful flash the towering cliff was revealed, so clear, so alarmingly close, its face drenched by spray and foam which rose from the frenzied combat of jagged rock and boiling sea.

"Pull for your lives or we'll be dashed to pieces!" Andraemon roared.

Nesa and Areon summoned up every last ounce of strength and pulled for all their worth. But the winds howled even louder, conspiring destruction, and the waves surged, intent on sucking the tiny vessel to its doom. In desperation Areon spoke to his heart within:

"The door of death is open wide. Is it a curse the gods have fixed upon us? Must it all end in this? Why? Why? We have overcome so much, we fought so hard!"

A second thunder-clap rent the air. Little Teg broke free from Osban's grasp and sprang to the bow, barking fearlessly. A huge wave struck the vessel hard, turning it this way and that; another – even more monstrous – came bearing down from behind. Still the dog barked, mindless of his peril.

"Come back here, Teg, you crazy animal!" Osban cried out. The dog did not respond, but barked ever more noisily.

"Rinja would never do this to me," Osban complained aloud as he crawled on hands and knees towards the animal. There was a terrific shudder as the wave hit, sending water cascading in on top of him, drenching him to the skin. "Blasted dog!" he cursed to the wild winds. He stood up now, feeling strangely unafraid.

He reached out and grabbed Teg by the scruff of the neck. With that the lightning flashed and he saw the rock – less than a spear-throw away, jagged, low in the water, sharply angled like the fin of a shark. He screamed a warning. Andraemon threw himself back on the steering oar. The boat careered past the rock, escaping disaster by a hair's breadth.

Water dripping from his face, Osban sat down with the dog in his lap and stroked him gently in gratitude. The boat sped onwards, at last clear of the headland.

By and by the storm eased off and passed away: the waves bowed, the winds ceased to howl, the rain melted away and peace returned to the heavens above.

Only then did Andraemon give the order to spread the sail.

"The sea, the sea – the free and glorious sea!" shouted Nesa for joy, stretching her arms wide.

Areon took a long deep breath of relief. And for the first time that day – for the first time in many a long day – he smiled.

The moon at last declared itself, appearing out from behind the ragged clouds to lay a silvery path before them. Urged by wind, wave and oar the boat surged ahead, vanishing into the night.

Up on the island ridge, Megnor's eyes glinted in the moonlight as he spoke to his men: "I saw them come this way. They are around here somewhere. I want every hill, every valley, every cave searched, not a rock left unturned till we find them."

Chapter 23

That road to the horizon was endless, the night seemed to go on forever. By and by Nesa and Osban, unable to fight their exhaustion any longer, lay down on the sheepskin rugs, pulled blankets around themselves and fell into a peaceful slumber. The dog and the lion settled down at their feet and they too were soon lost to the world.

But sleep would not fall upon Areon's eyelids this night. While the little boat fled downwind he sat watching the white turmoil of waters that rushed in retreat from the bow, and gazed at the moon and stars above that advanced with him in flight. Now and then he looked at the Sword which lay unsheathed on the bench beside him, delighted to behold its gleaming blade and twinkling hilt. He knew then that all of this was real and not a dream.

Nor did Andraemon sleep – though it seemed to him as if he were in a dream. As steadfast as the stars above, he stood at the steering oar, listening to the song of the sea as he watched, waited for the first hint of a new day.

"What made you change your mind?" Areon asked of him.

"About coming with you?"

"Yes."

"This made me change my mind," said Andraemon, slapping his hand on the steering oar.

"I don't understand."

"I speak of this boat," said Andraemon. " I once told Nesa of my two friends and of how they tried to escape?"

"She told me. They were captured and put to the sword."

"This is what the Achaeans claimed and I had no reason to doubt it. However, I met a fisherman one day who told me of the events of that night. He had been at sea, he said, and witnessed the chase. My brave friends in their little boat had no chance of shaking off the swift Achaean galley which had taken up pursuit. As the galley closed in on them, he saw them make one last desperate gamble. They leapt from the boat and tried to swim ashore. I can only guess that they hoped to hide out on the island, then cross to the mainland and hope for the best."

"A desperate gamble, right enough."

"Yes, a hopeless last throw of the dice, something that could only have ended in failure... But now I'm no longer so sure."

"Why? Why do you say that?"

"Perhaps they escaped, perhaps not – who knows. But what I do know is that this boat which you have found and rebuilt is that same boat of theirs. It became clear to me after Nesa talked of it again the other day. Just think, it lay there all those years, waiting to be found by you."

"That's a powerful omen," said Areon.

"A good omen, I agree," said Andraemon. "When I understood the meaning of it, I knew I had to come with you."

"And so you're here."

Andraemon smiled broadly. "And so I'm here."

When the blue of the eastern sky finally softened and the stars began to fade, Nesa awoke. She sat up, wiped the sleep from her eyes and stretched like a cat. "I really needed that sleep. I was so tired," she yawned.

"You slept like a log. And Osban didn't even snore once, I'm glad to say," said Areon.

"Come, let us eat," spoke up Andraemon. "You must be hungry."

"Starving," answered both.

Then Andraemon opened the big cloth bundle he had brought with him and laid out before them such foods that made their mouths water: fresh bread, wheat cakes and honey, cucumber and soft cheese, melon and apples."Help yourselves," he said and from a jug he poured cool, creamy milk into four cups.

There was a stirring and Osban sat up, eyes closed, yawning. A flicker of puzzlement crossed his face but was quickly banished with a smile. "For a moment I didn't know where I was – thought I was back at the hut."

"I knew we wouldn't have to wake you," smiled Areon.

"Look what Andraemon has for us," said Nesa between mouthfuls. "You had better come and get it."

In the wink of an eye Osban was up and seated next to them.

"What a feast!" he enthused, rubbing his hands in glee.

"A feast for the free. May it be the first of many," said Andraemon, raising his cup to them.

"The first of many," vowed the Trojans and they emptied their cups. Then they set upon the food. They ate ravenously, with Osban, in particular, making short work of the wheat cakes and honey, washed down with cupfuls of milk. Never had food tasted so good, all agreed.

Areon noticed that Nesa for the first time was wearing the three amber beads around her neck. "You'll be able to finish that necklace at last," he remarked.

"I thought I'd never see the day," said Nesa.

"What will be the first thing you do?"

"When we get home? As soon as this boat pulls into the shore I'm going to jump off and start running, and I'll run all the way to Troy – all the way! – so they better have the Gate open because I'll not stop until I come to our door."

"Yes, I'll do the same."

"Imagine, that little brother of mine is already over two years old. He'll have changed so much," she said. "I just can't wait to see him and give him a big hug."

"Think of the shock they'll all get when we appear."

"And the next day – as soon as it's light on the very next day – I'm going straight down to the stables and I'm going to saddle up the fastest horse there-"

"Oh yes!" agreed Areon.

"And I'll ride like the wind across the plains."

"I'll come with you."

"And I'll ride forever..."

"All the way to the slopes of Mount Ida! That sounds perfect, Nesa. We'll come with her, won't we Osban?" They turned to Osban, but he only half-nodded in response.

"And what would you like to do when you reach your home-land, young Osban?" Andraemon asked.

"I don't know," Osban shrugged. It seemed as if a shadow had suddenly descended upon him. "I suppose I'll have to go and find my dog, that's all. He's had nobody to care for him all this time..."

He stood up and turned to the sea. Nesa and Areon glanced at each other.

"But what about all the people who'll turn out to welcome you?" Areon asked out of the blue.

173

"What do you mean? No one will be turning out to welcome me."

"They will."

"They will not."

"They will, when they hear that you are the one who brings home this," said Areon taking up the Sword and scabbard. "Here, it's yours." He held it out to his friend.

A trace of a smile crossed Osban's face. He took the sacred weapon. "So Nesa told you about it."

"She did. You're a proper rascal – and a proper thief to boot."

"So you keep telling me."

"You'll be a true hero, Osban," Nesa told him. "The trumpets will sound, the banners will fly, they'll carry you shoulder high through the city – just think of that."

"So you think it will be like that?" he asked with a thoughtful expression.

His question seemed to ask more than intended, and they fell quiet for a moment, unable to ignore the uncertainty, the fear of what lay ahead of them. It was Andraemon who answered then:

"It will be as you say, Nesa. Fortune will favour the brave, you need have no fear."

The words re-assured them.

A golden glow behind the misty mainland mountains heralded the rising of the sun. The new day was finally upon them.

Then Areon lay back and stretched himself out on the sheepskin rug. He could feel the tiredness now washing over him like a wave. Nesa took up a few pieces of meat to feed Kaela and Teg. Osban went to the bow, the Sword slung by his side. He stood there proudly, while the boat rose and fell and ploughed onwards through the restless sea.

As the first rays of gold flooded the world, a flock of little birds came flying low over the water, screeching shrilly to one another.

"Areon, look at the birds," called Osban.

"Little Black Caps – that's what we used to call them," said Andraemon. "They are flying south for the winter."

"In a hurry too, like us," added Nesa.

Kreer-er kreer-er ki -ki-ki shrilled the birds as they flight-dipped or hovered or boldly dived into the waves.

"Quick, Areon, look at them," called Osban again.

But Areon had fallen into the soft arms of sleep and was already drifting away on the current of his dreams. And the rise and fall of the boat was the motion of his chariot, the call of the birds was the creaking of its wheels, the sheepskin rug he clutched were reins that seemed so taut. And he was riding now up to the open Gate... there his father stood, a spotted leopard's skin thrown round his shoulders. There his mother waited, and beside her his two brothers, and gathered around them the familiar faces of his friends, his neighbours, his people, all of them waiting to bring him home.

Watch out for another great book from
Blackwater Press
"Stanley"
by
Peter Gunning

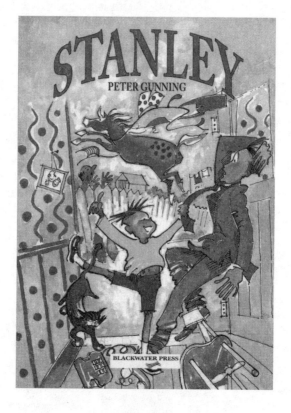

To look at Stanley, one might have been of the opinion that he was just
another normal young boy. There, unfortunately, one would have been
very much mistaken. Stanley was very, very different......
Stanley tumbles headlong from one hilarious exploit to another.
Wherever Stanley is, trouble is never far behind!